Enid Blyton

The Little Witch-Dog

...and other stories

Printed and bound by CPI Group (UK) Ltd, Croydon, CR0 4YY

Bounty Books

Published in 2015 by Bounty Books,
a division of Octopus Publishing Group Ltd,
Carmelite House
50 Victoria Embankment,
London EC4Y 0DZ
www.octopusbooks.co.uk

An Hachette UK Company
www.hachette.co.uk
Enid Blyton ® Text copyright © 2011 Chorion Rights Ltd.
Illustrations copyright © 2015 Award Publications Ltd.
Layout copyright © 2015 Octopus Publishing Group Ltd.

Illustrated by Georgina Hargreaves.

ISBN: 978-0-75373-050-8

A CIP catalogue record for this book is available from the
British Library.

Printed and bound by CPI Group (UK) Ltd, Croydon, CR0 4YY

CONTENTS

The Little Witch-Dog

There was once upon a time a little puppy who was bought by a witch. He was black and white, fat and very merry. But he hadn't lived long with the witch before he became thin and sorrowful.

The Pernickety Witch had bought him to guard her cottage from the goblins, the trolls and the dwarfs who very often came to steal her spells. Now the puppy, to whom the witch gave the ugly name of Snooks, was afraid of the goblins, trolls and dwarfs, for they were very ugly, made terrifying noises whenever he appeared, and shouted that they would turn him into a dog-biscuit and throw him to the birds.

So poor Snooks was unhappy and ran away whenever he saw anyone coming. Then the Pernickety Witch would beat him and cry, "What's the good of my buying you to chase away goblins, dwarfs and trolls when you run away as soon as you see one? You are a stupid, worthless animal, and if you don't do better I will turn you into a ball and throw you up to the moon!"

Well, what a terrible threat that was! The poor puppy didn't know which was worse – to be turned into a dog-biscuit and given to the birds – or turned into a ball and thrown up to the moon. He was really very frightened and miserable.

Another thing he didn't like at all was that he had to live with Cinders, the witch's fierce black cat. Cinders thought

Snooks was a stupid animal and whenever the puppy ran by, she stretched out her sharp claws and scratched him. So it was no wonder that the little puppy grew thin and sorrowful.

One day the Pernickety Witch called to the puppy, "Snooks! Snooks! Where are you, Snooks? Come here at once, Snooks!"

Snooks, who was having a little nap after carrying firewood for Cinders all the morning, woke up at once and ran to the witch.

"Now, Snooks," she said, "just listen to me. A pixie called Tiptoes is coming here this morning to fetch some washing for me. But I am really going to catch her and keep her for a servant, because Cinders doesn't cook as I like, although she keeps the house quite well for me. So I want you to go to the gate, as soon as Tiptoes is safely through it, and see that she doesn't get away when she knows what I am going to do with her. She is sure to try to run off home, and you must bark at her and snap at her ankles so that she will not dare to open the gate to go home."

Snooks turned quite pale. He loved the

pixies and elves, for they had always been kind to him, and he couldn't bear to think that the witch was going to play such a dreadful trick on one.

"I can't do it!" he said. "No, I can't, Mistress!"

"What!" cried the witch, in a rage, and she cuffed him on the head. "Don't dare to talk to me like that, you naughty little dog! If you don't do what I tell you, I'll throw you up to the moon, as sure as eggs are eggs."

Snooks ran off, trembling. Whatever was he to do? He couldn't, *couldn't*, help to keep a pixie prisoner! But what could he do?

"I don't care, I shall not help the Pernickety Witch!" he barked to himself. "As soon as I see the pixie I shall bark at her very loudly, so that she is afraid of coming in the gate. Then, if she can't come inside, she can't be taken prisoner!"

So he lay down by the gate and watched for Tiptoes. He soon saw her coming up the hill, a little creature in blue, treading lightly on her tiptoes and humming a little song.

As soon as she came to the gate Snooks began to bark. "Wuff!" he cried. "Wuff, wuff, wuff! *Wuff!*"

The pixie stopped and looked frightened. "Let me come through the gate," she said to Snooks.

"Wuff, wuff! Go away quickly!" barked Snooks. "The witch is waiting to catch you and turn you into her servant. Wuff, wuff, wuff!"

The pixie was frightened and ran away at once, helter-skelter down the hillside. The witch, who had heard Snooks barking,

but hadn't heard what he said, came rushing out in a great rage.

"You stupid, silly, little dog!" she cried. "I told you to bark at the pixie if she ran away from me – not before she was through the gate!"

"Snooks told the pixie you meant to turn her into a servant," said Cinders, the big black cat, who had been sitting on the wall all the time.

The Pernickety Witch gave a scream of rage and ran at Snooks. "I'll throw you up to the moon!" she shouted.

Snooks was full of fear and ran away down the hill as fast as ever he could. The witch tore after him. He soon came to the small cottage where the pixie Tiptoes lived. She was mixing a pail of whitewash, ready to paint the cottage. Snooks jumped right in to the pail and out again – and dear me, you would hardly have known him! Instead of being a little white and black dog, he was pure white all over, even his ears and the tip of his nose!

"Save me!" he barked to the pixie. "The witch is coming to turn me into a ball and throw me up to the moon."

10

"Lie down on the mat and I'll pretend you are my dog," said the pixie. So when the witch came running up, there was Snooks lying down pretending to be asleep on the mat, a little white dog from nose to tail. The witch called out loudly to the pixie.

"Have you seen a little black and white dog go by here?"

"No dog has passed by my cottage," said the pixie, truthfully. "Hey, little dog, have you seen a black and white dog pass by?"

"No, Mistress," answered Snooks and he closed his eyes again and pretended to go to sleep.

The witch made an angry noise and ran off. But when the whitewash had worn off Snooks's coat, as it did in three days, the witch heard that Tiptoes had a black and white dog and came running down the hill to see if it was Snooks.

But Snooks had seen her coming and he went hurriedly into the garden shed, where a big sack of soot was kept, and jumped right into it. When he came out he was a sight to see! He was pitch-black from head to tail, and nobody in this world would ever have thought him to be Snooks! He ran to his mat and lay down, pretending to be asleep.

The witch came running up and called to the pixie, "Pixie! I've heard that you are keeping a little black and white dog here, called Snooks. Where is he?"

"Look round and see for yourself!" said Tiptoes, hanging out her washing on the

line very busily. "See, there is my little black dog on the mat. Ask him if he has seen Snooks. He is sure to know."

"Wuff!" said Snooks, opening one eye. "I have not seen Snooks."

The Pernickety Witch looked at the pixie closely. "It is a strange thing," she said, "but last week you had a white dog. Now you have a black one. Is it the same dog?"

"It may be, and it may not be," said the pixie, coolly. "It's none of your business, Witch. If I choose to change my dog's coat whenever I like, it is nothing at all to do with you. Perhaps next time you come he will be black and white like your Snooks!"

The witch went away, grumbling loudly. It wasn't very long before she heard that the pixie no longer had a little black dog, for, of course, the soot had worn off in a short while, and she came running down the hill again.

This time Snooks was his own colour, and he lay on the mat as bold as brass. The pixie had told him just what to do.

"Is that the same dog as you had last week and the week before?" asked the witch, pointing with her skinny finger at Snooks.

"Exactly the same dog," said the pixie. "I told you he might be black and white next time you came, and he is!"

"I believe he is my dog!" said the witch, suddenly, peering closely at Snooks.

"You are quite wrong," said Tiptoes. "He is mine. He belongs to me."

"Prove it then!" said the witch.

"I will!" said Tiptoes. She turned to the dog and called, "Whiskers, Whiskers, Whiskers!" At once he came to her and jumped up in delight.

"There!" she said. "He knows his name. It is Whiskers. Now you call him by your name and see if he comes."

"Snooks, Snooks, Snooks!" shouted the witch. But the little dog didn't even look at her. "No," he thought, "I am Snooks no more. I belong to no witch. I am Whiskers, and I belong to Tiptoes, who loves me."

"*Snooks*!" yelled the witch, in a rage, quite sure that the little dog really was hers. "If you don't come to me at once I'll turn you into a ball and throw you up to the moon!"

Once that threat would have frightened the puppy, and sent him cowering to the witch's feet. But now, well-fed and well-loved, he really was a different dog, and all he felt when he heard the witch's threat was a fierce flame of anger, so that he rushed to her, snarling and showing his teeth. The witch was frightened, and backed away. The puppy went after her, snapping and growling.

"He's come to you, Pernickety Witch!" shouted the pixie, laughing. "Do you want him? Is he your dog? You can have him if you like!"

"*Gggg-rrr-rrr!*" growled the puppy, and the witch rushed up the hill in terror.

"He isn't my dog, I don't want him!" she cried. The pixie sat down on a stool and laughed till she cried. When Whiskers came back to her he frisked round her joyfully.

"Well, well," said Tiptoes, patting him, "the witch may be clever and know all the spells in the world, but a little whitewash, a little soot, and a trick or two have defeated her, Whiskers! Will you be my dog now, and look after me well?"

17

"Wuff, wuff!" barked Whiskers, joyfully. And that, as I am sure you guessed, meant "I will!"

The
Sensible Train

Fiona-Mary is very puzzled. You see, something very surprising happened, and she doesn't know whether it was a dream or whether it was real. I must tell you, and see what you think.

Well, the toys in the playroom were always up to tricks every night. The teddy bear built towers with the bricks and knocked them down over the rabbit whenever he came by. The sailor-doll rolled the ball at the toy soldier and knocked him over every time. The white dog shut the black dog's tail in the cupboard door and made him yell.

That was the sort of thing they did. But one night they got a shock.

They all got up on to the table to watch the two goldfish swimming in their bowl. The goldfish didn't like the toys at all, because the toys used to press their noses against the outside of the bowl and make rude faces at the goldfish. This was really very frightening indeed.

Now the yellow-haired doll wanted to see in at the top of the bowl, so she stood up and looked in. She was wearing a pretty bead necklace that had come out of a Christmas cracker – and just as she leaned over the water, this necklace broke!

All the beads fell into the water! How upset the doll was! She began to cry and squeal, and all the toys wanted to know what was the matter.

The teddy bear immediately said he would get the beads for the yellow-haired doll. He leaned over the bowl and put in a long arm, meaning to scoop up the beads from the bottom. But one of the goldfish swam at his paw and tried to bite it. The teddy bear gave a yell and fell head-first into the water!

There he stuck, head in the bowl and legs waving wildly in the air.

"Pull him out, pull him out!" cried the rabbit. But when the toys tried to do this, the bowl half tipped over, and the toys

knew that they would spill water and fish
if they pulled any harder.

They were frightened and climbed down
quickly from the table.

"What shall we do, what shall we do,
what shall we do?" they kept saying. But

they did nothing at all, while the poor teddy bear was half drowning in the goldfish bowl, and the fish were nibbling at his ears.

Now the railway train, who hadn't been able to climb up on to the table, was very upset when he heard about the teddy bear. He liked the teddy bear, who often drove him round the playroom at night.

"We must do something!" cried the train, clanking all his carriages. "Quick! Quick!"

But nobody could think what to do. Then the train, who was very sensible, gave a loud whistle and said, "Well, if you can't do something, Fiona-Mary will! I'm off to tell her!" And before the toys could stop him, he had unhitched his carriages and rushed out of the room, across the passage, and into Fiona-Mary's bedroom!

And this is where Fiona-Mary comes into the story. She woke up, of course, for no one can sleep with a clockwork train rushing round and round the room, whistling loudly. As soon as she sat up, the train rushed out of the bedroom, across the passage, and back to the playroom.

It knew very well that Fiona-Mary would follow it in surprise!

She did. She jumped out of bed and ran in astonishment to the playroom.

"Train! Did you really come into my bedroom?" she asked. "Who wound you up? Who ... ?"

And then she saw the poor teddy bear still struggling in the bowl of water! She ran to the table at once and jerked him out. He gasped and spluttered, and couldn't say a word.

She squeezed the water from his fur

and rubbed him with a towel to dry him. "Whatever do you want to go and swim in the goldfish bowl for?" she said. "What a silly you are!"

All the toys sat quite still and didn't say a word. Even the train had run into a corner and was quite still too. They were afraid of waking the grown-ups. Fiona-Mary yawned, rubbed her eyes, and went back to bed.

In the morning she awoke and remembered what had happened. "But it couldn't have happened!" she said. "It was just a dream. I know it was!"

And she was quite, quite sure it was. But the funny thing is – the teddy bear's fur was still damp, and the yellow-haired doll's beads were in the goldfish bowl! Now what do you think of that? Fiona-Mary simply doesn't know what to believe!

Where Was
Baby Pam?

Baby Pam was nearly two years old, and she could walk all over the place. Billie, her brother, and Susie, her sister, were very proud of her. So was her mother. She was such a happy baby, and everyone loved her.

Now one day, when the sun was shining brightly in the kitchen, Mother began to bake some cakes. Baby Pam watched her. She watched the sunshine too, coming in at the doorway.

She walked to the door and looked out. Her mother was busy and didn't miss her. She put one little foot out of doors and then the other – and in a moment she had gone from the kitchen to look for the sunshine.

In a few minutes Mother looked round to see where Baby Pam was. She wasn't there! Mother looked under the table. She wasn't there, either, hiding from her mother.

"Oh, dear," said Mother, "where has she gone?"

She ran to the door and looked out. She couldn't see the baby anywhere. Billie and Susie were playing among the bushes at the end of the garden, Rover was lying in his kennel, half asleep, and Puss-Cat was on the wall, washing herself. Wherever was Baby Pam?

"Billie! Susie!" called Mother. "Is Pam with you?"

27

Billie and Susie came running up the garden.

"No!" they cried. "We haven't seen her. Wasn't she in the kitchen with you, Mummy?"

"Yes," said Mother, looking worried, "she was. But I suddenly missed her and now I can't find her anywhere. It's time for her morning sleep, too. Wherever can she have got to? Look all over the garden, there's good children!"

Billie and Susie ran all over the garden calling Baby Pam. "Pam! Pam! Baby Pam!" they called. But no little girl came running to meet them. It was very odd.

"Has she gone out into the street, do you think?" asked Billie. "The back gate is quite easy to open."

"Oh, go and look," said his mother. "I do hope she hasn't."

Billie ran to see – but there was nobody in the road at all. Pam wasn't there.

"No, she's not there, Mummy," said Billie, coming back. "She must be in the garden, then. But where? We've looked simply everywhere!"

"Have you looked in the garden shed?"

asked Susie. "Come on – let's look there. I remember hiding there once when I was little."

They ran to the garden shed and opened the door. It was quite dark inside. They called "Pam! Pam!" loudly – but no one was there. They shut the door and looked at one another in dismay.

"Isn't it funny!" said Billie. "She must be somewhere. She can't just vanish."

"You don't suppose the goblins have taken her, do you?" asked Susie.

"Of course not! Don't be silly. The

goblins never come here. I know! Perhaps she has gone out of the back gate and into Mrs Brown's next door. Let's go and ask."

They ran down the path and out into the road. They went through the next gate and knocked at the front door. Mrs Brown opened the door, and was very much surprised to see Billie and Susie looking so hot and bothered.

"Is Pam here?" asked Susie.

"No, my dear," answered Mrs Brown. "Dear, dear, I hope you haven't lost her."

"Yes, we have!" said Susie, beginning to cry. "Whatever shall we do? We've looked simply everywhere."

"Why don't you go and get Rover, your dog, to help you?" said Mrs Brown. "He could soon follow her footsteps and find her for you."

"Oh yes, what a good idea!" cried Billie. "Come on, Susie, let's go and call him."

They ran back home. As soon as they were in their own garden they called Rover.

"Hi, Rover, Rover! Come here!" they called.

Rover opened one eye and looked at them.

"Come on, quickly, Rover!" shouted Billie. "You're not tied up. Come on!"

Rover raised his head and yawned. Billie felt cross.

"Rover!" he cried. "Will you do as you're told! Come here at once. We want you to look for Baby Pam."

Rover pricked up his ears when he heard Billie say "Baby Pam", but still he didn't move. He didn't even get up. He just sat there, half in and half out of his kennel, blinking at Billie and Susie.

The children ran up to him and caught hold of his collar. "Don't you understand,

Rover?" they cried. "We want you to help us to find Baby Pam. She's lost."

They tugged at his collar to make him get out of his kennel – but he wouldn't budge. Instead, to their enormous surprise, he growled at them!

"Rover! You growled at us!" said Susie, astonished. "You've never done that before. Oh, you unkind dog! Get out of your kennel quickly. Mummy! Mummy! Come and get Rover out. He's growling at us."

Mother came running out, looking more worried than ever. She had hunted upstairs and downstairs but still there was no sign of little Pam. She took hold of Rover's collar and pulled him out of the kennel – and then she gave a cry of surprise.

"Look!" she said, pointing inside the kennel. "Do look!"

The children looked – and there, fast asleep on Rover's blanket, was Baby Pam, hidden in the kennel! She was very fond of the old dog and had gone there to play with him – and then had fallen asleep in his kennel!

"No wonder Rover wouldn't come out when you tried to make him!" said Mother. "He was guarding Pam. He knew she was safe in his kennel, and he couldn't understand what all the fuss was about. Good old Rover!"

Mother patted him and he wagged his tail hard. Then Mother gently lifted Baby Pam off the blanket and took her, still sleeping, to her cot.

"What a good thing she's found!" said Susie, very glad. "Let's go and tell Mrs Brown where she was after all. Won't she be surprised!"

And Mrs Brown certainly was!

She Stamped
Her Foot

Melanie had a dreadful temper. When she was in a rage she went red in the face, shouted – and then stamped her foot!

"Melanie! Please don't stamp your foot at me!" said her mother crossly. "No matter what you want, I shan't give it to you if you stamp like that. It's rude."

Melanie stamped her foot again. It wasn't a bit of good – she was just sent up to bed!

So after that she didn't stamp her foot at her mother any more – only at her friends. They couldn't send her to bed – but they didn't like her at all when she stamped her foot at them.

One afternoon Melanie went to pick blackberries in Farmer Giles's field. She knew where there was a fine hedge of them – and as they were the last of the autumn's feast of blackberries, she meant to have a very nice time!

But she found a little old lady there, picking quickly, and putting the big, juicy blackberries into her basket. Melanie stared in rage.

"I came to pick these blackberries," she said.

"So did I," said the old lady, still picking.

"I saw them the other day, and I said to myself that they should be mine and no one else's," said Melanie, going red in the face.

"How funny! That's just what I said to myself!" said the old lady, still picking hard.

Melanie stared crossly. "I want those blackberries!" she said.

"So do I," said the old lady. "You can share them, can't you?"

"You've picked all the biggest. You're greedy," said rude Melanie.

"What an unpleasant child you are!" said the old lady, staring at Melanie out of curious green eyes. Those eyes should have warned Melanie that the old lady was magic, for people with green eyes are

not the same as ordinary folk.

"You're not to talk to me like that!" said Melanie – and she stamped her foot. "You're not to, you're not to!"

"Don't stamp your foot at me, or you'll be sorry!" said the old lady, and her eyes looked rather fierce. But did Melanie care? Not she!

She lost her temper all in a hurry, and began to shout and stamp. "I want those blackberries!" (Stamp, stamp!) "I want those blackberries!" (Stamp, stamp!) "I want those blackberries!" (Stamp, stamp, *stamp*!)

The old lady looked at Melanie in the greatest surprise. "My dear little girl," she said, "you shouldn't have been a child at all. You should have been a pony! Then you could do all the stamping you please!"

"Give me those blackberries!" shouted Melanie, and she stamped so heavily on the grass that she squashed it flat.

"I don't mind horses stamping at me, but I won't have little girls behaving like this," said the old woman, and she waved a thin brown hand at Melanie. "Be a pony! Run away and stamp all you like!"

And then, to Melanie's enormous dismay, she found that she was no longer a little girl, but a small brown pony with a white star on its head! She had four legs and a long tail!

She stamped with her forefoot on the grass, and opened her mouth to shout – but she neighed instead:

"Nay – hay – hay – hay – hay! Nay – hay – hay – hay – hay!"

"Well, if you want hay, go and get it," said the old lady, going on with her picking. Melanie was frightened by her horse-voice and ran away round the field. Oh dear, this was dreadful! She was a pony – fancy that, a pony! She couldn't speak like a little girl. She couldn't pick blackberries, for she had no hands. She could still stamp, and she could wave her long tail about – how very, very frightening!

Melanie wanted to go home, so she ran to the field gate. But it was shut. Melanie stamped her foot, and the old lady laughed.

"Stamp away! I always love to see a horse stamping with its hoof – it's right for horses to paw the ground! Stamp all you like, little pony, and enjoy yourself!"

But Melanie wasn't enjoying herself one bit. Supposing the farmer came by and put her between the shafts of a trap to take people for rides? Suppose he wanted to ride her? He was such a big, heavy man.

And what about her food? Would she have to eat grass?

Melanie put her big pony-head down to nibble the grass to see what it tasted like. It was horrid! She still had the tastes and feelings of a little girl although she had the body of a pony! Whatever was she going to do? Why, oh, why had she stamped at that old woman?

Just then George, John, Lucy and Rob came into the field. "Look!" cried Rob. "A new pony! Let's ride him!"

Melanie was full of horror. What – let those children ride on her back? Never! She ran away to a corner of the field, and the children followed.

The pony stamped her foot at them, and the children laughed. "He's like

Melanie!" they cried. "He stamps his foot just like Melanie!"

Just then the children's mother came along and called them. "Come out of the field, children. There's no time to play before tea. Come along."

Tea! Melanie felt hungry. How she wished she could go home to eat cakes, and jam too. But what would her mother say if a pony came running into the house?

Still – she would go home. Perhaps her mother would know her even though she was a pony. Melanie cried a few big tears out of her large pony-eyes. She cantered out of the gate that the children had carelessly left open, and went down the lane to her home. The door was open. The pony cantered inside – and there was her mother, laying the tea.

"Good gracious! A horse coming to tea!"

41

said Melanie's mother. "I never heard of such a thing! Shoo! Shoo! Go out at once!"

Melanie went right into the room and put her big pony-head on her mother's shoulder. Tears ran down her big brown pony-nose.

"Well, look at this!" cried her mother in greatest amazement. "A pony crying on my shoulder! Poor creature, what's the matter? Now, pony, don't be silly," said her mother, pushing it away. "Do you think you're a little dog or something, trying to get on my knee? You'll be borrowing my handkerchief to wipe your eyes next! Dear, dear, I don't understand this! I must be in a dream."

A voice spoke from the doorway. "No – you are not in a dream. That is Melanie – but she stamped her foot at me, so I changed her into a pony for a time. Horses may stamp when they please, but not children!"

"Oh dear, oh dear!" cried Melanie's mother, putting her arms round the pony's neck. "Now I understand what this poor pony wants. Old woman, you are magic! Change my little girl to her own shape,

She Stamped Her Foot

43

please! I am sure she will never, never stamp her foot at you again!"

"Will you ever stamp your foot again, Melanie?" the old lady asked the pony. It shook its big head at once. The old woman waved her hand – and lo and behold! – the pony disappeared, and there was Melanie, looking rather small and scared.

"Goodbye," the old lady said to her. "Remember that only horses stamp – so be careful you don't change into one again. You never know!"

She went out with her basket of blackberries. Melanie looked at her mother.

"Don't let me stamp my foot any more!" she wept, glad to find that she didn't neigh this time.

"Well, you must try and remember yourself," said her mother. "I can't tell your feet what to do!"

Melanie laughed through her tears. "I'll try and remember," she said. "I don't want to eat grass any more – and you don't want a pony stamping about the kitchen, do you, Mummy?"

All the same I hope I'm there if Melanie

ever does stamp her foot again – it would be so surprising to see her change into a pony!

Tinker and
Balloon-Face

Jennifer hung the big red balloon in her bedroom. It had a long string and hung down, swaying to and fro because it was so light. Jennifer had been to a party and every child had had a balloon.

The toys stared at the big balloon. They had never seen one before. The balloon had a face painted on it, and the face smiled and smiled. The toys rather liked it.

But they were afraid of the balloon and not one of them went near it, not even the toy lion, who was the boldest of the lot.

Jennifer went off to school. The toys were left alone in the bedroom. The balloon swung gently to and fro, because the window was open and a little breeze came blowing in.

Someone jumped in at the window. The toys looked at the someone in dismay. It

46

was Tinker, the next-door cat. The toys didn't like Tinker. He sometimes came in and stole the milk out of the milk jug. He chased the clockwork mouse all round the room. And once he had rolled a skittle over and over so long that the skittle had felt ill for a week.

"There's Tinker!" whispered the lion to the teddy bear. "Where's the clockwork mouse? Quick! Tell him to hide inside the brick-box."

"I hope he doesn't scratch off my new hat," said the doll. "He's a horrid cat. I wish he didn't keep coming here."

"Hello, toys!" said Tinker looking round. "You don't seem very pleased to see me! Say hello!"

"Hello, Tinker," said all the toys obediently.

Then Tinker caught sight of the big balloon swaying in the breeze. He saw the smiling face on the balloon and he thought it was another toy.

"I didn't hear you say hello!" Tinker said rather fiercely to the balloon. The balloon-face smiled away, and said nothing.

"Say hello or I'll smack you!" said the cat, crossly. The balloon swayed a little and grinned hard. It didn't say a word, of course.

"Now look here!" said Tinker, seeing that all the toys were laughing at him. "Now look here – you've got to be polite to me! I'm Tinker, the king of all the cats round here! I've bitten the ears of more cats than anyone else – and I can bite your ear, too!"

"He hasn't got one!" said the lion.

Tinker glared at the lion. "Don't speak unless you're spoken to!" he said. He turned back to the balloon. "What's your name?" he said.

The balloon didn't answer. Tinker spat at it angrily and the balloon swayed a little more. The face went on smiling and Tinker felt angry. "Take that smile off your face!" he said. "If you don't, I will! Stop grinning at me like that!"

The balloon went on smiling. Tinker suddenly hit out with a paw, and the balloon swung right back and then bobbed forward and bumped Tinker on the nose.

Tinker felt a little alarmed. He backed away a bit and the lion laughed loudly. Tinker ran at him and he dived into the toy cupboard and hid under the big kite there.

Tinker walked away from the cupboard looking so fierce that all the toys trembled. The clockwork mouse felt safe in the brickbox though, and shouted after him, in his squeaky voice:

49

"Yah, yah! You're afraid of the balloon-face! It's laughing at you! It thinks you are a silly cat!"

Tinker hissed in rage and looked all about for the clockwork mouse. But he had bobbed down safely in the brick-box and could not be seen. Tinker walked to the balloon again.

"You may think it's funny to bob about and grin like that," he said, "but it isn't! It's silly. You be polite and tell me your name, and I won't smack you any more."

The balloon didn't say a word, which wasn't surprising because it never had and never would. The wind blew in at the window and swung it against Tinker's ears.

"Don't do that," said Tinker fiercely. "Are you trying to bite my ears? Keep away or I'll scratch you!"

"Ho, ho!" laughed the toys. "The balloon isn't afraid of you, Tinker! You're afraid of old balloon-face!"

"I am not!" said Tinker. "I am afraid of nothing, not even of the great big dog across the road. He runs away when he sees me."

"Oh, fibber!" cried the doll. The balloon swung up into the air in the wind and came down on Tinker's tail.

"How dare you try to pull my tail?" said Tinker, swinging his long tail angrily from side to side. "Stop grinning like that, I tell you. It's rude. If you don't stop I'll scratch you!"

The balloon-face went on smiling broadly. Tinker lost his temper and lashed out with his right paw, all his sharp claws sticking out spitefully.

One of the claws went into the big

balloon. *Bang*! The balloon wasn't there any more! Only a bit of red rubber hung down from the string.

Tinker leaped high into the air. "I'm shot! I'm shot! Help me, I'm shot!" he cried.

But the toys had all dived into the toy cupboard and shut the door when they heard the loud bang. They sat and shivered inside, wondering what had happened to the smiling balloon. It just said "Bang!" and disappeared. It was most extraordinary.

Jennifer came back from school at that moment and heard the bang. She ran into her bedroom, and saw Tinker and the burst balloon.

"You bad, wicked cat!" she shouted at

him, almost in tears. "You've burst my balloon."

Tinker jumped out of the window in fright, and the toys heard him wailing outside in the garden. "I've been shot, shot, help, help, help!"

But nobody helped, and Tinker fled home and hid himself behind the sofa

trying to find out where he had been shot. But he couldn't.

"He won't come back again!" said the lion, poking his head out of the cupboard.

He didn't. Jennifer took down the balloon string and bit of rubber and threw them sadly away. She knew what had happened but the toys didn't.

"Where did balloon-face go to?" they kept asking one another. "He said 'Bang!' and went. Where did he go to?"

Perhaps Jennifer will tell them, or maybe she will bring home another balloon. I hope it won't go pop, don't you?

A Jolly
Thing to Do!

"Mummy, will you read to us after tea?" asked Peter.

"I can't, darling. The cold I've got has given me a sore throat and made my voice go croaky," said his mother. "I'll play with you, if you like."

"I don't want a game," said Jean. "If you can't read to us I want to make something, Mummy. Can't we make something?"

"Yes, if you like," said her mother, and she thought hard. "Listen, if you'd like to go out into the wood this afternoon, while I have a rest, and bring back whatever you find, we'll make something that you can take to school with you tomorrow!"

"Oh, Mummy, what?" asked Peter.

But she shook her head and laughed. "How can I tell you what we shall make until I know what you will bring back?" she said.

"But Mummy, it's November, and there's hardly anything to find in the woods," said Jean. "No flowers, no anything."

"Well, if you can't bring back anything, we can't make anything," said her mother. "You must see what you can find, even if it's only a few twigs!"

That afternoon, when their mother had gone to have a rest, Peter and Jean put on their coats and wellington boots, took a basket, and went out. They walked down the lane to the woods and shuffled through the dead leaves that lay thick on the ground. Peter saw a fir-cone and picked it up.

"Look," he said, "here's something – a nice dry cone."

"We can't make much with that!" said Jean. "But cones burn nicely on the fire. We could take some home for that, if you like."

So they filled their basket with cones, big and small. Then they came to a little thicket of oak-trees. There were still some old brown leaves on the

trees, rustling in the wind.

"We might find some acorns underneath," said Jean. "Let's look."

So they hunted about and found quite a lot. "They're nice," said Jean, "so smooth and oval. I like them. We could give them to the pigs at the farm, if we can't make anything with them. And here are some acorn-cups too, Peter."

"What are those brown balls on the oak-trees?" said Peter, and he pointed to where hard round balls, like brown marbles, grew here and there on the bare branches of the oak.

"Those are oak apples," said Jean. "I learned about them in school this term. They're called galls. They're not the fruit of the oak, Peter, they're just growths caused by insects."

"How strange," said Peter, and he picked some off the twigs. "They look exactly as if they might be the fruit of the oak – though I know those are acorns. We'll take some of these home too, shall we, Jean?"

So into their basket went the oak apples and rattled there with the acorns and cones.

Then Jean found some red haws on the bare hawthorn tree. "Look!" she cried, "do you remember the white may blossom we saw here in the summer? Wasn't it lovely? Now the fruit has come and it's these round red berries the birds like so much. Shall we take some sprays home with us? They're so pretty."

"We'll take some twigs too," said Peter, and he broke some here and there from the trees. "We can put them into a vase if we don't use them."

"It looks as if it's going to rain," said Jean, looking up at the sky. "We'd better get back quickly before we're soaked."

"But we haven't many things to take home," said Peter. "What can Mummy make with these? Nothing much!"

"I expect she'll be able to," said Jean. "I felt a drop of rain then. Come on Peter, before it pours down."

They ran home and got in just before the storm broke. They emptied their basket on to the kitchen table and then took off their coats and boots. It wasn't quite teatime, so they took their books and read. They didn't want to make a noise because their mother was still having her rest.

At teatime they showed her what they had brought home from the woods.

"Not very much, Mummy," said Jean. "But really there wasn't much to find. In summer there would be heaps of things."

Mother looked at their collection of fir-cones, acorns, oak apples and the rest.

"Quite a nice lot of things!" she said. "We shall be able to make some fir-cone girls! They are easy to make and look comical when they're done."

"Oh, let's start quickly!" said Jean, who loved making things. "Mummy, how do you make them?"

"Finish your tea first," said their mother, so both children hurried up and finished it. Then they went to the table where they had put their things. Mother gave them a large sheet of newspaper to spread over the table so that they wouldn't make too much mess.

"Now," she said, picking up a fir-cone, "this shall be the fir-cone girl's dress. It looks nice and frilly, doesn't it?"

So it did! Then she picked up a brown oak apple. "This shall be her head," she said. "Have you got your paint-boxes out, children? You can paint white eyes, a white nose and a white mouth on the dark oak apple, for a face."

Peter and Jean chose a nice round oak apple each. Soon they were busy painting funny little faces on them.

"Mine's finished," said Jean, holding

hers up. "She's smiling."

"Good," said Mother. "Now we'll stick the head firmly on to the bottom bit of the cone – where the stalk is. Your stalk is too long, Peter. Cut it off till it's level with the bottom of the fir-cone."

"How do we put the head on firmly?" asked Peter.

"We can glue it on," said his mother. "Or, if you like, you can bore a hole in the neck of the fir-cone, and a little hole under the chin of your oak apple face, and put a bit of matchstick into the holes

61

to hold them together, so that the oak-apple is joined very firmly indeed to the cone. Put a spot of glue where they join as well."

Peter managed to put his oak apple head on the fir-cone body by means of a bit of match driven into the little holes he made, but Jean glued hers on without bothering about holes or matchstick.

"Now we've got body and head," said Mother. "What about legs and arms?"

"Twigs, of course," said Peter; and he began to break one up into bits for arms and legs.

"Make a little forked bit come just where the hands should be," said Mother. "It looks more real then. Now, you can stick them on with glue, if you like, or bore holes in the twigs and the cone and join them with pins or bits of matchstick, whichever you like."

The children worked hard. Soon they had legs and arms finished.

"I wish mine would stand up," said Jean.

"We'll make stands for our fir-cone girls, then," said her mother; and she fetched an old cork from the cupboard. She cut three pieces from it. "There," she said, "now we have stands for our girls. Bore holes in your bits of cork, and then stick the twig-legs into the holes, dabbing a spot of glue where they meet."

Peter managed his beautifully, but Jean broke one of the legs, and had to get another bit of twig.

"That's right, Jean," said her mother. "You've got a fine little twig, this time, with a bent bit that looks like a knee. Now put it very carefully into the cork."

"Our fir-cone girls have got dresses, arms, legs, heads and faces," said

Peter, "and something to stand on. What about hats?"

"Oh, these acorn-cups would do for hats!" cried Jean; and she rummaged about in the acorns for the little cups some of them had been in. "Look, Mummy, aren't these cups pretty, with their tiny stalks? They look as if someone had carved a pattern all round them."

Jean stuck an acorn-cup over the oak apple head. It fitted beautifully.

"My fir-cone girl looks very smart," she said. "Try one for yours, Peter. Here's a nice one."

"I want mine to have hair first," said Peter. "I don't want her to be bald. Mummy, what can I have for hair?"

"Well, you try and think of something yourself," said his mother. Peter looked all round. He saw some yellow wool in the workbasket – just the thing for hair!

"Can I have some of that yellow wool?" he asked. "I could snip short bits off and glue them on my doll's oak apple head."

"Yes, you can both have some of the wool if you like," said Mother. But Jean didn't want yellow wool. She thought she

would have black wool. Soon both children were neatly snipping short bits from the wool. Then they glued them on to the dolls' heads.

"Now to put on their acorn hats!" cried Jean, and popped hers on. The dolls looked very good. The children were delighted!

Jean saw the red hawthorn berries she had brought home with her. "They'll do for buttons down her dress," she said, and dabbed glue down the front of the fir-cone frills. She squeezed the berries on, and they looked like red buttons.

"Mine won't have buttons," said Peter. "I'll run a little ribbon under the scales of the cone round the middle and make a sash for my fir-cone girl."

They were finished. Mother and Peter and Jean stood them up on the mantelpiece and smiled to see the funny fir-cone girls there.

"Mine's called Fanny Fir-Cone," said Jean.

"Mine's Alice Acorn," said Peter.

"And mine's Olive Oak Apple," said their mother. Then they all laughed.

"You must take them to school with you tomorrow," said Mother, "and show the other children. You can easily teach them how to make them."

So the next day Peter and Jean took the fir-cone girls to school and set them on the class table for the others to see.

"How lovely!" said Miss Brown, their teacher. "I believe they would sell very well at our school Christmas Fair, Peter and Jean. They are most amusing, and cleverly done, too. Could you make some more, do you think?"

Well, of course, they could – and they did, too. And at the school Christmas Fair Peter and Jean had a table all to themselves, full of fir-cone girls they had made. They did feel proud.

"Aren't we lucky to have a mother who can make things like this with us?" said Jean. "We did have fun."

I expect your mother would make some fir-cone girls with you, too, if you asked her. Wouldn't you like to make a fir-cone family?

The
Walking Bone

Bonzo and Tinker were two puppies who lived in the park-keeper's cottage with Mr Tidy-Up, the park-keeper. Mr Tidy-Up's job was to plant out the flowers in the park, weed the flower-beds, water them, and, of course, to tidy up everything nicely. No crisp packets, no sweet bags, no bottles, no bits of paper were allowed to lie about on the grass or paths from one day to the next.

You might think that Bonzo and Tinker would do their best to help their master, Mr Tidy-Up, for he was good to them, giving them bones and biscuits each day, and he had made a fine box for them, with a little rug inside. But no – the puppies were a terrible pair, untidy, lazy and mischievous.

The things they did! You wouldn't

believe them! One day Mr Tidy-Up had very neatly labelled all the new plants in the big flower-bed by the park gates – and those naughty pups rooted up the wooden labels as soon as his back was turned and chewed them all!

Another time they watched him planting the daffodil bulbs – and they thought they were some special kind of bones! So as soon as poor Mr Tidy-Up had gone to his tea the puppies dug up all the bulbs and bit them to see what they were like. Mr Tidy-Up gave them a good telling-off for that – but two days later they behaved just as badly as ever.

When they began to bury their bones all over the park beds, Mr Tidy-Up was cross.

"Now listen to me, Bonzo and Tinker," he said. "I don't mind you burying your bones – but I WILL NOT HAVE you digging them up again! You've got such bad memories you don't remember where you put your bones, and you dig up half the park before you find anything. So just remember – bury your bones if you like – but DON'T DARE to dig them up again."

Well, you might as well talk to the kettle on the stove as talk to Bonzo and Tinker. They just didn't care for anyone. If they wanted to dig up bones, they would dig them up, so there!

"You know, Bonzo," said Tinker, one sunny spring morning, "I'd like to dig up that fine, juicy bone we stole from the butcher the other day. Where did we bury it? There was a nice lot of marrow in it we didn't have time to finish."

"Didn't we bury it by the park gates, where the daffodils are?" said Bonzo.

"I don't think so," said Tinker. "I think we buried it in the round flower-bed by the duck pond."

"Or was it in the bed of tulips?" asked Bonzo, thinking hard. "Well – let's go and try in all those places."

Off they went. They tried in the bed of yellow daffodils and dug up about fifty before they decided their bone was not there. Then off they went to the round flower-bed by the duck-pond, and after frightening two ducks nearly out of their lives, they dug up half the bed and then decided that they certainly hadn't buried the bone there at all.

"I say – did we put it by that old mossy wall over there?" said Tinker, suddenly. "I seem to remember putting it there. Let's

try there before we dig up the tulip bed."

So off they went and dug hard in the wet bed at the foot of the old mossy wall. And they found something big and hard!

"It's our bone!" cried Bonzo, pleased. "Look! Isn't it a big one! I'd forgotten it was so big, hadn't you, Tinker? Let's take it to the woodshed and we can chew it there alone."

So between them they carried the big, heavy thing to the woodshed and put it down on the floor. They lay down, panting, their little red tongues hanging out of their mouths.

They looked at the bone – and to their enormous surprise it moved! Yes, it did – it really did!

"Did you – did you see it move?" Bonzo asked Tinker, very much afraid.

"I d-d-d-d-don't know," said Tinker, staring at the big, brown thing in fright. It moved again.

"Oooooooh!" yelped Tinker in a dreadful fright.

"It's got legs!" barked Bonzo, all the hair on his neck standing up in terror.

"And now it's grown a head!" yelped

Tinker, who was hardly able to stand up, he was so frightened.

It was quite true. The big bone had moved, put out four thick legs, and then thrust out a head in which were two little eyes! It wasn't a bone, of course. It was a tortoise that had buried itself in the bed by the old mossy wall to sleep quietly through the winter. But the two puppies really did think it was a bone, and they were dreadfully frightened to think that their bone should grow a head and legs and look at them like that!

The tortoise wanted to get outside in the sunshine. It wanted to go and find a lettuce to eat. So it began to walk slowly towards the two puppies, meaning to go out of the door.

The dogs sprang up in fear. They yelped wildly and then, their tails between their legs, they fled out of the woodshed yelping: "The bone's after us! The bone's after us!"

The tortoise was surprised to see the puppies behaving so strangely. But he was old and wise and nothing upset him. So he went quietly on his way to find a lettuce.

The puppies ran indoors and curled up together, shivering, in their cosy box.

"We have been very naughty dogs all our

lives," said Tinker. "This is a punishment to us. It is worse than anything."

"Perhaps all our bones will come alive and grow legs and heads," said Bonzo, trembling as he remembered the tortoise putting out its little head and looking at him.

"I shan't be naughty any more," said Tinker. "I shall be a good dog from now on."

"And I'll never, ever go digging up bones or anything else as long as I live," said Bonzo.

And from that day the puppies became two of the best dogs in the world, – they were good, obedient, tidy and hard-working. Mr Tidy-Up doesn't know why and he is very much puzzled about it. I'd very much like to tell him about the Walking Bone, wouldn't you?

A Basket
of Acorns

The oak-tree shook its leaves in the sunshine. The wind blew and the branches waved about. Some of the ripe acorns dropped to the ground below – *bump-bump-bump*!

A little squirrel came frisking over the ground and saw them. "Acorns! Nice nutty acorns!" he chattered in delight. "Plenty for me to eat, and plenty for me to hide away!"

A little dormouse heard the squirrel, and came running out of his nest in the branches.

"Go away!" he squeaked, angrily. "These are my acorns! This is my tree!"

"Why is it your tree?" said the squirrel in surprise. "It doesn't belong to you."

"It does, it does!" squeaked the dormouse. "I live in it and so it is mine."

"Well, I often live in the branches, and once I had my nest here, so it is mine too!" chattered the squirrel. He gathered up some acorns in his little paws, and the dormouse ran at him in a rage.

They made such a noise that a big jay came flying down. He screeched loudly and made both the squirrel and the dormouse jump. "Don't screech like that," said the squirrel in fright. "I've told you before, Jay, that you have a dreadful voice."

"I shall screech as much as I want to," said the jay. "Ha! Acorns! So that's what you were quarrelling about! Good! I

like acorns! I didn't know there were any ripe yet."

"These are my acorns!" said the squirrel.

"No, mine I tell you!" squealed the dormouse.

"Well, they are mine too," said the jay. "This oak-tree is mine. I have sat in its cool green shade for three years. It is my tree, and it grows its acorns for me and not for you!"

Then what a noise the three of them made, quarrelling about the fallen acorns. The squirrel no sooner picked up an acorn than the jay pecked it out of his paw – and when it rolled on the ground the little dormouse darted on it and held it! The squirrel made little barking noises, the dormouse squeaked, and the jay screeched at the top of his voice for all the world as if someone were hurting him dreadfully! But he always sounded like that. He really had a very harsh voice!

Three children came along through the trees, carrying a basket. They heard the noise of the jay, the dormouse and the squirrel, and they wondered what the matter was. They hurried up to see.

"Oh, look!" said Amy. "There is a squirrel – and it is quarrelling with a dormouse and a jay. I wonder why!"

"Let's look and see!" said Ann. "Come on, you two!"

They ran up to the tree. The squirrel at once bounded up the trunk and disappeared among the leaves. The jay flew off. The dormouse ran into his nest in the tree.

"They've gone!" said Amy. "Oh look –

this is what they are quarrelling about
– acorns!"

She held one up. "Isn't is pretty? Shall
we gather a basketful to take home to
Grunter the pig? He will be so pleased to
have them. He does like acorns."

"Yes – do let's take some home," said the
others. So they gathered up a big basketful
of acorns. It was fun to hunt for them in
the mossy ground beneath the spreading
branches of the great oak-tree. The wind
in the leaves said

"Sh-sh-sh!" all the time, as if it were whispering a secret.

"Now let's play hide-and-seek," said Amy. She hid behind the tree, and the trunk was quite big enough to hide her. When Johnnie came round to find her she slipped to the other side, like a squirrel!

When the children had gone home, the squirrel, the dormouse and the jay went to the ground again to hunt for acorns – but not one could they find! The children had taken them all!

"What a pity!" sighed the squirrel. "We need not have quarrelled – there were plenty of nuts for us all. Now we have none. It serves us right!"

"Sh-sh-sh!" said the oak-tree. "I will send some acorns down for you all tomorrow, if you promise not to quarrel! I have plenty more getting ripe!"

So they promised – and tomorrow they will all eat together like friends. I would like to see them, wouldn't you?

Tabitha's Trick

Mr High-and-Mighty was in a fine temper. He stamped up and down his study, and roared at the top of his voice.

"So the people of this village think I oughtn't to sell Breezy Hill, do they! I'd like to know what it's to do with them! Breezy Hill is mine, and I shall sell it if I want to!"

"But, my dear," said Tabitha, his gentle wife, "all these years the people of the village have looked upon Breezy Hill as their own – they have picnicked there, picked blackberries and nuts there, gone primrosing there in the springtime, and loved it very much. Now, if you sell it to that horrid man, Mr Sly, he will build himself a nasty big house there, put up walls and fences and hedges – and nobody else will ever be able to enjoy Breezy Hill."

"And why shouldn't I sell it if I want to?" roared Mr High-and-Mighty again. "I need the money."

"Oh no, my dear, you don't," said Tabitha. "You have too much already. Don't be greedy – let the people have Breezy Hill. They will be so grateful to you if you do."

Mr High-and-Mighty banged his big stick on the ground. "I don't want to make the people grateful! I don't care tuppence about them."

"Well, I care," said Tabitha. "Do you want to make the villagers hate you? Do you want to make them really angry?"

"I don't care if I do!" said Mr High-and-

Mighty, and he put on his big hat with the long feather. "I am going straight away now to Mr Sly to tell him he can buy Breezy Hill. So there!"

"Oh dear!" sighed Tabitha. "Well, I'll come with you, just in case you change your mind."

Tabitha ran upstairs. She felt about in her wardrobe and brought out a very large bag of sweet, round peppermints. She was very fond of them and always kept a lot in her wardrobe. She put on her hat and shawl and went downstairs, carrying the bag of peppermints with her.

Mr High-and-Mighty was already marching down the path. Tabitha hurried after him. They went down the street together.

As soon as they passed some children playing in the road, Tabitha dropped two or three peppermints. The children saw them and ran up at once. Tabitha dropped a few more. The children were thrilled, and ran after Mr High-and-Mighty and Tabitha in delight, beckoning to all the children they passed. Soon there were about twenty children following behind.

Some men working in the road looked up in surprise as they saw the crowd of children. "What's up, I wonder?" said one. "Let's go and see."

So they followed after the children – and of course every one was most astonished to see such a crowd.

"Come on! Let's see what's happening!" cried Mr Jinks, Mrs Feefo, and Dame Goody – and they all ran to join the crowd following Mr High-and-Mighty and Tabitha. Tabitha kept dropping peppermints all the time, so the children ran close to her, excited and pleased.

More and more people joined the crowd, wondering what was happening. They made such a noise of chattering that Mr High-and-Mighty looked round. When he saw the enormous crowd behind him, he was surprised and alarmed.

"Tabitha, look!" he said.

Tabitha looked. "Dear me!" she said. "What a crowd of people."

"Why do you suppose they are following us?" asked Mr High-and-Mighty anxiously.

"Well, dear, how should I know?" said gentle Tabitha, though she did very well know why the children came.

"Tabitha – you don't think – you don't think they are following me to see if I am going to Mr Sly's, do you?" asked Mr High-and-Mighty anxiously. "You don't think they are getting angry with me?"

"Well, I know I would feel angry with you if I were a villager who loved Breezy Hill and hated that horrid Mr Sly," said Tabitha.

"Oh dear!" said Mr High-and-Mighty,

who wasn't nearly so brave as he looked. "Oh dear! Perhaps I'd better go home, and see Mr Sly another day."

So he went down a sidestreet and turned towards home. Tabitha smiled to herself. She did not throw out any more peppermints behind her, so gradually the children left – and the grown-ups, seeing that nothing was happening, went back home too.

Mr High-and-Mighty was very glad indeed to see nobody following him.

"Dear, dear, it really does look as if the villagers were following me to see if I was going to Mr Sly's," he said. "What do you suppose they would have done to me if I had gone into Mr Sly's house, Tabitha?

Do you think they would have been very angry?"

"Oh, furious, I should think," said Tabitha. " Now, my dear, why don't you give up this greedy idea of selling Breezy Hill to that nasty Mr Sly, and couldn't you instead give it to the people? They would be so pleased."

But Mr High-and-Mighty felt much braver now that he was at home with only his wife. He frowned at her and banged his stick on the floor again.

"Once and for all, no!" he cried. "I shall sell Breezy Hill to Mr Sly – and I'll do it tomorrow, you see if I don't!"

Tabitha said nothing. She went upstairs and looked inside her wardrobe. There were no more peppermints there – and she only had a few left in her bag. She had better get something else for tomorrow.

She slipped out and went to the grocer's. She bought a large bag of tiny round biscuits, each with a little dab of coloured sugar on them. The children would love those!

The next day Mr High-and-Mighty put on his big hat again, took his stick, and

went out, nose in air, to sell Breezy Hill to Mr Sly. Tabitha trotted along beside him, holding her large bag of biscuits. Mr High-and-Mighty was far too grand to notice what she was doing.

When they passed some children, Tabitha dropped a few of the sugar biscuits. Up ran the boys and girls like dogs after bones! More children joined them as Tabitha dropped the biscuits – and soon the grown-ups came along too, following the children, and wondering what was happening. Before Mr High-and-Mighty had got to Mr Sly's, he had a long train of children and grown-ups behind him, chattering and calling.

"What's up?" called the grown-ups to one another. "What's up?"

Every one trotted along to see, for a crowd makes people run to join it. Soon half the village was behind Mr High-and-Mighty – and suddenly he turned round and saw it again.

"Oh my!" he said in dismay. "There are all the people again, following me about. Wife, this is dreadful. How do they know I'm going to Mr Sly's?"

"I'm sure I don't know," said Tabitha. "Hadn't you better go home again before anything happens?"

"What do you mean – before anything happens?" said Mr High-and-Mighty nervously. "Do you think the people might get angry with me? Oh dear – just look at the crowds! Yes – I had certainly better go home." He turned to go home – and just round the corner whom should he meet but old Mr Sly himself! Mr Sly was ugly and mean, very rich indeed, and very anxious to have the beautiful Breezy Hill all for his own.

"Good morning!" he said to Mr High-and-Mighty, who wasn't at all pleased to see him just then. "I want to talk to you about selling me Breezy Hill."

Mr High-and-Mighty looked round him anxiously. Breezy Hill was the last thing he wanted to talk about in the street, with such a crowd around him.

"Er – another day, perhaps," he said to Mr Sly. But Mr Sly wasn't going be put off like that. He took Mr High-and-Mighty's arm and pointed with his stick to Breezy Hill.

All the crowd at once knew that he meant to ask Mr High-and-Mighty to sell him the hill. They began to talk excitedly to one another. Mr High-and-Mighty became more and more nervous.

"I can't talk about it now," he said. "Not with all these people about."

"Why not?" asked Mr Sly in surprise. "What does it matter about the people? But, dear me – what crowds there are! What are they following you for?"

"Er – well, Mr Sly – you see, it's like this, Mr Sly," said Mr High-and-Mighty, lowering his voice, "I'm afraid the people don't like the idea of me selling Breezy Hill to you. They keep following me about like this – and I'm very much afraid that if they hear me selling Breezy Hill to you, they will set about us both and beat us!"

Mr Sly turned pale. He was rich and
powerful, but, like Mr High-and-Mighty,
not at all brave in his heart. Tabitha
dropped a few more biscuits and the
children rushed around, shouting in glee.
Mr Sly didn't like the shouting. A child
bumped into him, and he was sure that
someone was just about to hit him hard.

"Well, I don't want your silly old Breezy
Hill," he said suddenly in a very loud but
rather trembly voice. "I wouldn't dream of
buying it. Horrible place!"

Mr High-and-Mighty was surprised to
hear this and very angry. He thumped his
stick on the ground.

"Breezy Hill is a lovely place!" he
shouted.

"It's not!" yelled Mr Sly.

"It is!" yelled Mr High-and-Mighty.
"And I tell you this, Mr Sly, that if you
don't like it, well, hundreds of people do!
Talking like that about our lovely hill,
indeed!"

"Pooh!" said Mr Sly rudely.

"And pooh to you!" roared Mr High-and-
Mighty, losing his temper altogether and
dancing about on the pavement in rage.

"Tell the horrid creature you'll give Breezy Hill to the village!" said Tabitha suddenly. "That will serve him right!"

"Yes – good idea – I will!" snorted Mr High-and-Mighty. He shouted after Mr Sly, who was stamping down the road. "I shall give Breezy Hill to the village, so there! The villagers like it, if you don't!"

The people around him heard this, of course – and they looked at one another in delight. What? Breezy Hill to be their own – and not sold to that nasty Mr Sly? How lovely! How generous of Mr High-and-Mighty! They began to cheer.

"Three cheers for Mr High-and-Mighty! Hip, hip, hurrah!"

Mr High-and-Mighty went red with

pleasure. He stood there, taking his hat off and bowing politely to every one. He felt marvellous. How fine it was to be generous! How wonderful it was to be cheered like this! What a good thing he hadn't sold Breezy Hill to that nasty Mr Sly!

He went home, followed by a cheering crowd. He was very happy indeed. "Well, Wife," he said, as he put his stick into the hallstand. "Well, Wife – isn't that splendid?"

"Oh, my dear, I am glad we can let the people have the hill," said Tabitha.

"We?" said High-and-Mighty, frowning.

"We, did you say? You had nothing at all to do with it, Tabitha. Nothing!"

Tabitha smiled and smiled – but she didn't tell Mr High-and-Mighty why. Wasn't she a clever little person?

In the Middle
of the Night

Harry was excited because he was going to stay with his Uncle Peter and Aunt Mary. He loved going to them, because Uncle Peter was such fun. He could play any game under the sun! He loved football and cricket and tennis, and he could run tremendously fast. Harry often used to boast about his uncle to the other boys at school.

"My Uncle Peter has a whole cupboard full of silver cups he has won for running and tennis and other things," he said. "You should see them! My Aunt Mary says it takes her two days to clean them when they have to be cleaned!"

"He'd better be careful a burglar doesn't come and steal all those cups!" laughed one of the boys. "Gosh, that would be a fine haul for anyone."

97

"Pooh! No burglar could steal them," said Harry. "The cupboard is tightly locked, and Uncle has a big dog."

But all the same, a robber did come and steal those silver cups! It happened while Harry was staying with his uncle and aunt too, so it was all tremendously exciting, and very upsetting. Uncle Peter, Aunt Mary and Harry had all gone out for a walk one afternoon, and Sandy, the big dog, had gone too, so the house was left quite empty.

When they all came back – what a shock for them! Someone had opened the

dining-room window, slipped inside and gone to the cupboard where the silver cups were kept. A pane of glass had been neatly cut out of the front, and every single cup had been stolen! Not one was left!

"There must have been two men," said the policeman who was called in. "One to keep watch, and the other to do the job. I expect they had two sacks. It's a wonder they got away without anyone seeing them!"

It was a very strange thing, but not a single person had seen two men about – not even one man had been seen!

The two men who were painting the house, who had been working outside all afternoon, said that no one had been about at all. It was most puzzling.

Uncle Peter was terribly upset to lose all his beautiful cups that he was so proud of. "They will all be melted down into silver," he groaned. "And that will be the last of them!"

Harry was very sad too. He did wish he could help find the thieves. But though he prowled round and asked everyone if they had seen two men with sacks, or one man with a sack, he couldn't find out anything at all.

So, after a while, nobody did anything more about it, and the police said they were doing what they could but they doubted if the thieves would be caught now.

Harry begged his uncle to lock the doors of the house very well every night. He was so afraid that the thieves might come again and steal his new aeroplane, or even his penknife, which was a very fine one he had had for his birthday. So Uncle Peter locked up every door and window, and told Harry not to worry.

One night Harry woke with a jump. He sat up in bed. Something had awakened him – what could it be? It was the very middle of the night, and everywhere was dark. Was it a noise that had awakened him?

He listened – and then he heard a sound – but it was not the noise he expected!

It was a pitiful wail from somewhere outside, and Harry's heart sank. He knew what it was – a rabbit in a trap in the field outside the garden. He had heard

that noise before, and it made him very unhappy. The sound came again and again.

"Poor little bunny," said Harry. "It's little soft paw is caught. Oh, how I hate those traps! The poor little thing will be in pain all night long, and so terribly frightened."

He lay down – but the sound still went on, a dreadful wail like a baby crying in the dark. Harry couldn't bear it. He was a kind boy, fond of all animals, and he hated to know that anything was being hurt.

"I can't stand this," said Harry. "I'm going to get up and go out into the field. Perhaps I can find the poor little thing and rescue it."

He pulled on his jeans and his sweater

and trainers. He groped about for his torch and found it in the cupboard. He slipped downstairs and out into the garden, switching on his torch to see the way he was going.

"Gosh, I hope there aren't any robbers about tonight!" thought Harry. "I shouldn't care to meet any! I forgot about them – oh, dear! Now I'm frightened!"

He stood in the garden in the dark, and wondered if he should go and call Uncle Peter. No, he might be cross. The rabbit wailed again and Harry forgot his fears.

"I'm not half so afraid as that poor little creature!" he said to himself. "I'm going on!"

Down the path he went, his torch throwing a beam of light in front of him. Slugs and worms slid everywhere, and a hedgehog hurried into the garden bed. It was strange to be out in the middle of the night.

Harry came to the gate at the bottom of the garden. It led into the field. It was locked, so he climbed over it. He stood in the field grass and listened. The rabbit cried again, and Harry went towards the sound. The animal was frightened when it saw the beam of light, and lay still. Harry had to hunt for a long time before he came across the trap, and saw the rabbit there, caught by its front paw.

Harry knew how to spring the trap. He had freed animals before, and it was only a matter of a moment or two before he had set the rabbit free. He looked

at the frightened animal, and whistled in surprise.

It was a pure black rabbit! Harry had expected to see the usual sandy-coloured wild rabbit – but here was a lovely creature.

"You must be a tame rabbit, escaped and gone wild again," said Harry. "I've a good mind to take you home with me and bathe that paw of yours. Then I might be able to find your owner and take you back. You will be safer in a nice hutch than running about the field."

The rabbit was very tame. It stayed by Harry and let him stroke it. He lifted it up and walked back over the field with the rabbit. It was awkward climbing over the gate, but he managed it. He got back home and took the rabbit into the bathroom.

He gently bathed the hurt paw. Then he bound it up. The rabbit let him do everything without a murmur, and seemed delighted to have a friend like Harry.

"Now I wonder what I should do with you?" said the little boy. "I know! I can put you in the box downstairs in the kitchen, the one Puss-Cat had for her kittens."

So the rabbit slept there for the night, with a board over the top of the box so that he could not jump out and use his hurt paw.

Uncle Peter and Aunt Mary were most astonished when they heard about the rabbit and how Harry had gone to get him in the middle of the night.

"You deserve a silver cup for that!" said Uncle Peter. "Weren't you afraid, Harry?"

"Yes, I was rather," said Harry, blushing red. "But I thought the rabbit must be more afraid than I was!"

Uncle Peter made a nice hutch for the rabbit, and he went to live there while his paw was getting better. Aunt Mary asked everyone she knew if they had lost a fine black rabbit, but nobody had.

"Perhaps I will be able to keep him for my own," said Harry. "He is such a dear, and so gentle and tame. He doesn't even run away when I put him on the lawn, Auntie."

"Well, let him loose sometimes, if you are there to watch him," said Uncle Peter.

"But don't let him eat my lettuces, will you?"

Soon the black rabbit was so tame that Harry let him out every day in the garden. His paw was healed, and he was very happy. Harry played with him each day and hoped that he wouldn't hear of anyone who had lost the rabbit. He did so want to keep him for his own.

And then one morning the rabbit disappeared! Harry had gone indoors to get a book, and had left him eating the grass on the lawn – and when he came back there was no rabbit to be seen!

Harry called him, "Bunny, Bunny, Bunny!"

But no rabbit came. Then the little boy began to look for him – and he soon found him! He had gone down to the bottom of the garden and was busy digging a burrow under the hedge there! Harry watched him. He saw how he scraped out the earth with his front paws and shot it out behind him with his back ones. When he thought the rabbit had done enough digging he picked him up and carried him back to the hutch.

Then he went to look at the tunnel the rabbit had made. He bent down and put his arm into it to see how far the rabbit had gone – and he felt something down there!

Harry took hold of it and pulled. It felt like a bit of sacking – and as he pulled, the boy heard a clinking sound. And at once a thought rushed into his head.

"I believe there's a sack buried here – with Uncle's cups in it!" he thought. "Oh, I wonder if it is!"

He pulled and tugged, and sure enough he was right. A big sack was buried there – and Peter saw at once that it was full of the stolen silver cups. The little boy stood and thought for a moment, and then he fetched a spade. Instead of digging up the sack, he put it back and filled the hole neatly to make it all seem as if no one had been there at all. Then he hurried in to tell Uncle Peter.

His uncle and aunt were most astonished.

"And, Uncle Peter!" said Harry, in excitement. "I've covered up the hole – and I thought if you hid in the shed

nearby at night, you could see who comes to get the sack – and then you will know who the thief is!"

"I've a very good idea who the thief is now," said Uncle Peter sternly. "I think it's the painters. But it's a good idea of yours, Harry, to hide in the shed and catch the thieves red-handed. I'll ring up the police and tell them. I shouldn't be surprised if they fetch the sack tonight, because they are finishing the job tomorrow – and no doubt mean to take the cups with them!"

The police were most interested in Uncle Peter's news – and two policemen were sent down that night to hide in the shed with Uncle Peter. Harry begged to be allowed to hide too.

"Oh, please do let me!" he cried. "It was my discovery. Do let me share in the excitement."

"Very well," said Uncle Peter. "You may. But you're to keep inside the shed all the time – you're not to come out at all, even when we go out and catch the thief."

So Harry promised, and that night he and Uncle Peter and the policemen all crept down silently to the shed. They slipped inside and sat down on some sacks to wait. There was a moon that night so it would be easy to spy the thief if he did come. The hedge was well lit by the moon, and Harry knew exactly where the sack was hidden.

In the middle of the night there came the sound of soft footsteps down the garden path. Someone was coming! Harry was so excited as he and the others peered out of the small window of the shed. They had cleaned it so that they might see clearly through it.

"It's Jones, the painter!" whispered Uncle Peter to the policemen. "Just what I thought! And listen – here's someone else!"

Another figure came quietly up and spoke in a low voice. It was the man who worked with him! So there had been two thieves after all! The police had been right.

The two began to dig. Soon they came to the sack and pulled it out. The painter threw it over his shoulder and the cups made a jangling sound.

"Now!" said one of the policemen. The door of the shed was flung open and out rushed Uncle Peter and the policemen. Harry had to stay behind as he had promised, but he did wish he could go and help too. But there was no need for his help. Jones, the painter, dropped the sack in dismay, and at the same moment one policeman clicked the handcuffs round his wrists.

His accomplice was caught by the other policeman. "He made me help him!" said the man.

"You can tell me all about that later," said the policeman sternly. Then the two were marched off to the police car, and Harry was told to go to bed.

All Uncle Peter's cups were put back in the cupboard, after Aunt Mary and Harry had spent two whole days in cleaning them. They were very stained and dirty from their stay in the damp sack. Uncle Peter was delighted to see them back,

and he stood a long time looking at them shining brightly in their glass-fronted cupboard. Then he turned to Harry.

"Well, Harry," he said, "it's all because of you that I got back these cups of mine! If you hadn't been brave that night and gone to get that poor rabbit – and if he hadn't dug in the garden and found that sack –

I'd have lost my cups for good! I shall give you another black rabbit to match yours, Harry, and a new hutch. You can take them home when you go, and I know they will be happy with you!"

Wasn't that nice of Uncle Peter? Harry was delighted! He has a fine new hutch now, and two fat and glossy black rabbits – and seven small baby rabbits besides! Isn't he lucky?

But he deserves his luck, because he was

kind and brave, the sort of boy that anyone would be pleased to have for a friend!

Mister Hoo-Ha's New Suit

Mister Hoo-Ha was a vain little gnome. He loved to have everything just a bit nicer than any one else, so that he could boast about it. He liked to have the shiniest mackintosh, the biggest umbrella, the tallest top hat, and the most pointed shoes. He liked to have the biggest cucumbers in his garden, and the highest sunflowers. He was that kind of person.

Nobody liked him very much, and they used to laugh at him behind his back. But Mister Hoo-Ha didn't know that. He thought that every one looked up to him and said he was the smartest gnome in Fiddle-Dee Village.

Ah! But just wait a minute, Mister Hoo-Ha. Pride comes before a fall, you know – so be careful!

Now one day the Smiling Witch thought

she would give a party. Every one loved her parties, for the Smiling Witch was a kind old dame, and liked people to have a good time. She often asked the Prince and Princess of Elfland, and the Lord of Feefo and the Lady of Fum, so the folk of Fiddle-Dee Village always put on their very best clothes when they went to the parties given by the Smiling Witch.

When Mister Hoo-Ha got his invitation card he was most excited. "I shall have a wonderful new suit made!" he said to

himself. "Oh, a marvellous one! I shall be smarter than anyone else! I wonder what I can have it made of. I should like to find something quite new. I think I will go off in the bus to the world of boys and girls and see if I can pick up anything there." So off he went in the bus.

When he got to our world, he found it covered in white snow, for there had been a snowstorm the night before.

Mister Hoo-Ha stared at the snow in delight and amazement. He had never seen snow before. He put out his hand and felt it. It was very soft.

"Just the thing for my new suit!" said Mister Hoo-Ha to himself. "Just the very thing! Pure white! No one will have pure white. And so soft! Like a duck's down. My, I shall be very smart and unusual this time!"

He took out his scissors and cut three and a half metres of snow. He rolled it up and packed it in a bag. Then he caught the next bus back to Fiddle-Dee Village and went straight to the tailor's.

The tailor was surprised to see such soft, white stuff. "It will be difficult to make up into a suit, Mister Hoo-Ha," he said.

"That's your business," said Hoo-Ha. "I pay you for doing that, don't I? Well, just get on with your work, then, and make me a fine suit – the finest you have ever made."

The tailor did his best. It was really very difficult, for the needle slid in and out of the snow, and until the tailor used a special frosty thread he could not seem to sew the snow together. But at last the

suit was made, and delivered to Mister Hoo-Ha's house.

"Good!" said Hoo-Ha, turning the soft, shining suit out of the box. "Very good! It looks lovely!"

When the night of the party came Mister Hoo-Ha had a bath, and then put on his vest. It was rather dirty and had some holes in it – for although Hoo-Ha was most particular about his suits and hats, he didn't mind very much about the things he wore underneath.

"After all, nobody ever sees those!" he said. "I can't be bothered to keep washing and mending my vests. So long as I am nice on top, it doesn't matter what I'm like underneath!"

So, even for the party, he put on his dirty and holey old vest. And then he put on his new snow-suit! My, you should have seen it! It was so soft, so white – and how it glittered! It was the loveliest suit ever seen in Fiddle-Dee Village.

Mister Hoo-Ha put on his new white hat to match and went off to the party. How he twirled his stick as he went along! How he stuck out his toes!

But the new suit was rather cold. It made Mister Hoo-Ha shiver. His nose turned blue with cold. His fingers could hardly take hold of his stick.

"It's a c-c-c-cold n-n-n-night!" said Mister Hoo-Ha, his teeth chattering.

The Smiling Witch greeted him kindly. Every one else had arrived, for Hoo-Ha always liked to come in last, because then, you see, everybody could see how grand he looked! The Smiling Witch took him by the hand and led him to the fire.

"You are cold, Mister Hoo-Ha!" she said. "Dear me, you are shivering! Come and warm yourself! What a wonderful new suit you are wearing! I have never seen anything like it before!"

"It certainly is beautiful," said everyone, in wonder. Mister Hoo-Ha felt very grand. He turned himself all round so that every one could see him.

"Yes," he said. "It's the very latest fashion. You ought to have some dresses made of it, Smiling Witch. It costs a lot of money, this stuff, but still, it's worth it."

Now this was a naughty story, for Mister Hoo-Ha had simply cut the snow off the ground for his new suit. But nobody knew that, so he just went on boasting for all he was worth. He still felt very cold, and he stood in front of the Smiling Witch's big fire, warming himself all over.

And then a strange and curious thing began to happen. Hoo-Ha's lovely new suit began to disappear! It turned into water and dripped off him! You see, it was made of snow – and so, of course, the hot fire melted it! Mister Hoo-Ha looked down in surprise when he felt something dripping down his legs!

"Your suit's melting! Your suit's

melting!" cried all the little folk. "Oh, look!"

There was no stopping it. It went on melting till it was all gone – and there stood poor Mister Hoo-Ha in front of the fire, with nothing on but a dirty and very holey vest!

"Why don't you mend your vest?" cried the little folk, in disgust. "What's the use of wearing grand things on top, if you're shabby underneath! For shame, Mister

Hoo-Ha! Look at your holey vest! You're nothing but a boaster, Mister Hoo-Ha! Go home and mend your vest!"

Well, that was the end of Hoo-Ha's boasting. It was a long time before he went to a party again – but when he did, he went early, and sat in a corner and he wore clothes just about the same as other people, no finer and no smarter. And underneath he was neat and clean, so you see he had learned his lesson! Poor Mister Hoo-Ha!

The Sailor-Doll's Chance

The sailor-doll sat on the shelf and sighed so much that he made quite a wind in the air.

"Whatever's the matter?" asked the blue rabbit, just below. "You make quite a draught with all your sighing."

"I'm sad because I have to live indoors and never go out in a boat or a ship although I'm a sailor-doll," said the doll. "I'm dressed like a sailor, and if you read what is written round my cap you will see it says H.M.S. *Glorious*, which means that I belong to Her Majesty's Ship *Glorious*. Well, where is my ship? Where is the sea? Here I am, wasting my time sitting on a shelf, instead of doing my work, sailing a brave ship!"

The blue rabbit agreed. It did seem a waste of time for a sailor-doll – especially as Polly, the little girl he belonged to, didn't like him very much and never played with him. She only liked her baby-doll and her pretty long-haired dolls. She didn't like gentlemen dolls at all.

So the sailor-doll had a very dull time. But one night he got his chance. Just listen!

It was a bright moonlight night and the sailor-doll was sitting up on his shelf watching the other toys playing on the floor. He was so dull and miserable that he didn't want to join in. He just watched. As the toys played about, something happened! A small fairy flew in at the top of the open window and shouted to the toys.

"Help! Help! Can one of you come down to the river and rescue little Sylfai? We were sitting on a leaf sailing down the stream, and the wind upset it. I flew off – but Sylfai fell in – and her wings are wet so she can't fly out. She will drown! Oh, please help!"

The toys stopped playing – but not one of them knew what to do. Nobody could swim – except the yellow plastic duck, and

he knew he wouldn't be any use because he would have to float where the river took him.

But the sailor-doll jumped up at once. "I will rescue Sylfai!" he shouted. "Where's the little boat Polly had when she went to the seaside?"

He scurried to the box where bricks and little toys and odd things were kept. He hunted through them all, throwing everything out in a great hurry – and at last he found the little blue boat. Then he looked for its oars and found them with the tea set. Polly had been using them for teaspoons.

The sailor-doll was little but strong. He put the oars in the boat, put the boat on his shoulder, and ran to the door with it. He slipped quietly down the stairs and climbed out of the kitchen window. He slid down the pipe outside, first throwing the boat down to the flowerbed below.

The little fairy picked up the oars for him. Once more he put the boat on his shoulder and, guided by the fairy, set off down the garden path to the river.

"Look! There's Sylfai, still struggling!" cried the fairy, pointing to the middle of the river. The sailor-doll put his boat into the water. He got into it and pushed off. He began rowing. He was very happy.

"I'm being a proper sailor for the first time!" he said. "And I'm doing something really worthwhile."

He rowed and he rowed. The river was strong and tried to take him away with it instead of letting him go to the struggling fairy. The sailor-doll found that it wasn't so easy to row as he had thought. It was very hard work.

His arms ached. His back felt as if it were breaking. He would never, never get to Sylfai! The other fairy flew beside him, begging him to be quick, quick, quick!

The sailor-doll panted and puffed. He was so hot that he felt as if he were on fire. He rowed and he rowed and he rowed – and at last he came near to the little fairy struggling in the water. But do you know, she was now so weak that she couldn't pull herself into the boat.

"Oh, whatever are we to do?" wept the little fairy, flying over the boat.

"Now listen to me," said the sailor-doll firmly. "Take hold of the boat, fairy, and hold it here if you can. I'll dive in and see if I can get Sylfai."

The fairy flew down and held the little blue boat as hard as she could. The sailor-doll dived into the water with all his clothes on. He could swim, of course, because he was a sailor. He swam up to the little fairy. He caught hold of her. He turned her on her back, put his hands under her arms, and kicked out hard with his legs. He knew this was a good way of life-saving people in the water.

But he was so tired, poor sailor! He had hardly any kick left. If the other fairy hadn't managed to get the boat near to

him he would never have got to it. At last
he felt the boat bumping gently against
him and he caught hold of it. With the
help of the other fairy he got Sylfai into
the boat, and then they all had a rest, for
nobody could move.

The river took them away. They floated
on and on and on – and at last the fairy
gave a cry of delight.

"The river has taken us to the shores of
Fairyland!" she cried. "Look!"

The sailor-doll sat up and looked. What a
beautiful sight met his eyes! The river was
lapping against a golden shore, and in the
distance, silvery in the bright moonlight,
he could see towers and spires and turrets,
gleaming and glittering. Fairyland!

It wasn't long before they were safely in
a fairy's cottage, drying their clothes. The
sailor-doll wondered however he could get
back to the nursery. But Sylfai put her
arms round his neck and hugged him.

"You're not to go back," she said. "You
must stay here and grow wings, and be a
fairy sailor. The Queen wants one to row
her across the river each week. Won't you
stay and ask for the job?"

So the sailor stayed, and he got the job. Now he is ferryman to the Queen herself, and you should see him rowing across the river in a golden boat, his new blue wings gleaming brightly. He is grand!

Polly often wonders where he has gone. Tell her, if she asks you.

Old
Mother Wrinkle

Old Mother Wrinkle was a strange old dame. She lived in an oak-tree, which had a small door so closely fitted into its trunk that nobody but Dame Wrinkle could open it. It was opened many times a day by the old dame, for always there seemed to be somebody knocking at her door.

The little folk came to ask her to take away their wrinkles. Fairies never get old as we do – but sometimes, if they are worried about anything, they frown or sulk, and then lines and wrinkles grow in their faces. Frown at yourself in the glass and see the ugly wrinkle you get.

Mother Wrinkle could always take away any wrinkle, no matter how deep it was. She would take a fairy into her round tree-room, sit her down in a chair and look at her closely.

"Ho!" she might say. "You've been feeling cross this week. There's a very nasty wrinkle right in the middle of your forehead. Sit still, please!"

Then she would rub a curious-smelling ointment on the fairy's forehead to loosen the wrinkle. Then she took up a very fine knife and carefully scraped the wrinkle off. She powdered the fairy's forehead and told her to go.

"But don't you frown any more," she

would call after her. "It's a pity to spoil your pretty face."

Now Mother Wrinkle had taken wrinkles away for two hundred years, and the inside of her room was getting quite crowded with the wrinkles. She didn't like to throw them away, for she was a careful old dame. She packed them into boxes and piled them one on top of another.

But soon the boxes reached the top of her room – really, there must be a million wrinkles packed into them. What in the world could Mother Wrinkle do with them?

Now the fairies did not pay her for taking away their wrinkles. Sometimes they brought her a little pot of honey, sometimes it was a new shawl made of dandelion fluff – but the old dame hardly ever had any money, and she needed some badly.

"I want a new table," she said, looking at her old worn one. "I would love a rocking-chair to rock myself in when I'm tired. And how I would like a pair of soft slippers for my old feet!"

She told the sandy rabbit this one day when he came to bid her good morning. He nodded his long-eared head. "Yes," he said, "you do want some new things, Mother Wrinkle. Well, why don't you sell those boxes of wrinkles and get a little money?"

"Sell the wrinkles!" cried the old dame. "Why, I'd love to – but who would buy them? Nobody! If people want to get rid of wrinkles they certainly wouldn't pay money to get some. That's a silly idea, Sandy Rabbit."

The rabbit lolloped off, thinking hard. He liked the old woman. She was always generous and kind. He wished he could help her. He talked to the pixies about it. He spoke to the frogs. He told the hedgehog. He spoke to the bluebell fairy – and last of all he met the little primrose fairy, and told her.

She listened carefully and then she thought hard. She had been very worried for the last fifty years because the primroses, which were her special care, had been dreadfully spoiled each spring by the rain. Whenever it rained, the wet clung to the leaves, ran down to the centre of the plant and spoilt the pretty yellow flowers. It was such a nuisance. She had been so

worried about it that Mother Wrinkle had had to scrape away about twenty wrinkles from her pretty forehead.

But now she had an idea. Suppose she took the wrinkles that the old dame had got in her boxes! Suppose she pressed them into the primrose leaves! Suppose she made them so wrinkled that when the rain came the wrinkles acted like little riverbeds and drained the water off at once, so that it didn't soak the leaves and spoil the flowers!

"What a good idea that would be!" thought the primrose fairy joyfully. "I'll try it."

So she went to Mother Wrinkle and bought one box of wrinkles. She took them to her primrose dell and set to work. The primrose leaves, in those days, were as smooth and as thin as beech leaves – but when the fairy began to press the wrinkles into the leaves, what a difference it made!

One by one the leaves looked rough and wrinkled. In the middle of her work the rain came down, and to the fairy's great delight the wrinkles acted just as she had hoped – the rain ran into them and trickled to the ground in tiny rivulets!

"Good!" said the fairy in delight. "Now listen, primrose plants! You must grow your leaves in a rosette and point them all outwards and downwards. Then, when the rain comes, your wrinkles will let it all run away on the outside – and your flowers will be kept dry and unspoilt."

Little by little the fairy gave wrinkles to every primrose plant, and they grew well,

till the woods were yellow with the flowers in spring. Mother Wrinkle was delighted to sell the old wrinkles. She bought herself a new table, a fine rocking-chair, and two pairs of soft slippers.

And now you must do something to find out if this strange little story is true. Hunt for the primrose plant – and look at the leaves! You will see the wrinkles there as sure as can be – delicate and fine – but quite enough to let the rain run away without spoiling the pale and lovely flowers.

The Gentle Scarecrow

Once upon a time there were two small robins. They had met one early spring morning in the old hedgerow and when the little cock robin swelled out his red throat and sang a song saying how beautiful the little hen robin was, she was so pleased that she said she would marry him and build a nest.

So they hunted up and down the hedgerow for a good place. At the bottom was a ditch full of dead leaves.

"These leaves would be splendid for making a nest," sang the cock robin.

"So will this moss!" sang the hen, pulling some out with her beak in delight.

"Look! Here is a fine hole in the bank!" trilled the cock, excitedly. "Shall we build here?"

The hen flew up and looked inside

the hole. It had been an old wasps' nest the year before. A tiny mouse had been inside and gobbled up anything that still remained. Now the hole was empty. It faced the right way, and was well-hidden under the overhanging hedge. The hen robin was pleased with it.

Together the robins built their nest. They wove a few tiny twigs together, they twisted in some grass roots, they brought green and brown moss to tuck in the cracks. The cock robin found nice dry leaves in the ditch and decorated the nest beautifully with them. When he had finished you could hardly see the nest at all, for it matched the ditch and the bank so well, with its moss and dead leaves!

"Now," said the little hen robin, happily, "I shall lay some eggs. Then we'll have some tiny robin chicks to love. Won't it be fun!"

But before she could lay any eggs, a dreadful thing happened! The farmer's son came along that way, looking for nests, because he wanted to collect eggs for himself. First he looked in the hedgerow and found a hedge-sparrow's nest with three blue eggs in and he took all those. Then he looked down on the bank and saw the little hen robin sitting close on her new nest.

"Shoo! Shoo!" cried the boy, unkindly. The robin flew off, frightened, and from a nearby bush the cock robin sang angrily at the horrid boy.

The boy bent down to see if there were any eggs in the robin's nest, and when he saw there were none, he flew into a rage. He kicked at the pretty nest and it flew to pieces! The bits of moss, the grass-roots and the dead leaves fell to the ditch below

– and that was the end of the little nest that had taken the robins a whole week to build.

The little birds were sorrowful. When the boy had gone they hopped around the place where their nest had been and grieved bitterly.

"It is such a good thing there were no eggs in it," sang the little hen robin. "Suppose he had taken them! Or smashed them! How sad we would have been then!"

"I don't like that boy!" trilled the cock. "Let us build our next nest in some place where he never goes."

So they hunted round once more – and then, in a field on the farm they found an old kettle with its lid gone. The cock perched near the hole where the lid had once fitted and sang to his mate.

"Here is a good place! This hole will take a nest very nicely! We shall be safe here. Come, let us bring moss and leaves, and build again in this friendly old kettle."

So once more the two little redbreasts began to build. How hard they worked! The days were warm, and the little hen was anxious to lay eggs and bring up her chicks. Soon the nest inside the kettle was finished. It was very cosy indeed. You could hardly see it unless you looked inside. Only some dry grass and a strand of moss peeped out of it, and when the hen robin sat inside just her beak could be seen.

She laid four pretty red-brown eggs. The two little birds were so pleased and proud. The hen sat on them all day long to keep

them warm, and the cock roamed about to find dainty titbits to bring to her. He sang to her, too, and she listened. When it rained she tucked herself down into the kettle and fluffed her feathers well out so that her precious eggs should not get wet.

Now one day the farmer himself walked over the field. He had planted seeds there, and the birds had been busy eating some of them. The farmer was very angry indeed. He clapped his hands at the rooks there, and shooed the jackdaws. But as he had no gun with him the birds cawed and took no notice.

"I shall put up a scarecrow," said the farmer, in a rage. "That will keep all the birds away! Drat them! Not one of those birds is an atom of good to a farmer!"

Well, of course, that's where he was wrong. It was true that some of his seeds were eaten, but dear me, if only he could have seen how many harmful grubs, beetles and caterpillars the birds ate too, how surprised he would have been!

He walked along by the side of the field, grumbling. When he came up to the kettle, the sun shone out and made it shine here and there, though most of it was very rusty. The farmer looked at it and frowned.

"How many times am I to tell those people not to throw their old kettles, saucepans and tins on my fields!" he shouted angrily. "I won't have it!"

He picked up the kettle. It seemed heavy so he looked inside – and as he looked, the little hen robin, who had been sitting on her eggs, flew out in a fright. She almost flew into the farmer's face and she made him jump.

"Another bird!" shouted the farmer, and he shook his fist. "It's got its nest in the kettle, too – well it can go and nest somewhere else!"

With that he threw the old kettle over

the hedge into the garden of one of the cottages nearby and stamped off, saying, "Yes, a scarecrow is what is needed, no doubt of that at all!"

The eggs in the nest fell out and were broken. The kettle crashed to the ground and the nest was spilled out in a heap.

The two robins were nearly broken-hearted. They sat close together in the hedge, and looked mournfully down at their smashed eggs.

"They were almost hatched," whispered the hen robin, in despair.

"First the farmer's son, and then the farmer!" said the cock robin. "Are we never to have a nest and eggs in safety? Wherever shall we build now?"

"I don't feel as if I want to build any more," sighed the little hen robin. But the cock nestled close to her and cheered her up. "We'll find a good place!" he sang. "Don't fear! We shall be lucky the third time!"

Now the next day along came the farmer and put up a most fearsome looking scarecrow in the middle of the field. It had a carved-out turnip for a head, an old hat, a raggedy coat and scarf and a pair of the farmer's oldest trousers. It had wooden sticks for arms and legs and really, when the farmer had finished putting it up, it looked for all the world like an ugly old man standing guard right in the middle of the field!

All the birds there were frightened. They really thought it was a friend of the farmer's, and when the wind blew the coat to and fro, they flew away in terror. The robins were frightened too.

"Do you think that horrible, ugly

creature will come after us and find our nest and eggs when we build and lay once more?" asked the hen robin, fearfully. "He is even uglier than the farmer himself."

"I will go and ask him if he means to harm us," said the cock robin, bravely. "If he says, yes, we will fly away to another place and build there."

So off he flew to the scarecrow in the very middle of the field. He perched on its hat and spoke to it.

"Do you mean to spoil our nests?" he asked.

The scarecrow looked at the little robin out of his big turnip eyes. The tiny bird saw that he had a kind face, though very ugly.

"Why should I want to spoil your nest?" said the scarecrow, in astonishment. "I wish no one harm. I would like to be friendly with all birds and beasts for I am very lonely out here all by myself, shunned by everyone. But no one ever comes to say how-do-you-do, or to wish me goodnight."

The robin looked at the scarecrow's gentle face in surprise. "You are not really the farmer's friend, then?" he asked.

"Oh, no," said the scarecrow. " He is a rough, bad-tempered man. I am sorry to have to work for him – but what can I do? I cannot get up and walk away, you know. Here I must stay, day and night, cold, lonely and miserable."

The cock robin called his little wife and told her that the scarecrow was a gentle, friendly creature, who would certainly not harm them or their eggs.

The hen sang her best song to the scarecrow and he was delighted. "Do build your nest somewhere really safe this time," he begged. "I should be so unhappy if I knew that once more your nest had been spoiled."

"I can't think where to build this time," said the cock robin. "I've hunted everywhere, and nowhere seems really safe."

For a few minutes the scarecrow said nothing at all – but suddenly his big turnip face lit up and he shook with excitement.

"Friends!" he said. " I know the safest place in the world for you! The very, very safest!"

"Where is that?" asked the robins.

"In the pocket of my coat!" said the ugly old scarecrow, his kind face still beaming. "No one would ever think of looking there, not even the farmer himself! Not a person in the world would guess that any bird was daring enough to nest in the pocket of a scarecrow! Oh, do build your nest there, little friends. You can't think how happy it would make me. I should no longer be lonely or unhappy."

The robins flew down to the coat and peeped at the pocket. It was a big one, and gaped open. It was really just exactly right for a nest! The robins stared at one another excitedly.

"The scarecrow's right!" sang the little

cock. "He's right! This is a good place, a safe one, where we can be unseen. Let us nest here!"

So they began to build their nest in the pocket of the scarecrow's raggedy coat. They filled it with soft moss, roots and leaves, and then the little hen robin cuddled inside and laid four more red-brown eggs.

How delighted the old scarecrow was! When the eggs hatched and the little chicks cheeped hungrily he almost twisted

his turnip head off, trying to look down to see what they were like! The old robins talked to him every day and sang their best song, for they were most grateful to him for his help.

One day the farmer's boy came along the field path, and as he went he looked along the hedge and the bank.

"Where did those robins build?" he said in a temper. "They must have built somewhere again, and I have never found their eggs, after all. I suppose that scarecrow has frightened them away. What a pity! I could have found their eggs and taken them."

"Did you hear that?" whispered the scarecrow to the two robins, who were closely cuddled inside his pocket, sitting over their young ones to keep them warm.

"Yes, we did!" trilled the robins. "You were quite right, scarecrow – this was the very safest place of all! If you are here next year we'll come and build in your pocket again!"

Won't the scarecrow be pleased if they do! He was sad when the two old birds and the four young ones said goodbye –

but they often go to see him, so he isn't nearly so lonely as he used to be, poor, gentle old scarecrow!

The
Two Dogs

Once upon a time there were two dogs. One was called Binkie, and the other was called Scamp. They often went about together, although Binkie didn't really like Scamp because he was such a mischievous sort of dog.

Now one day Binkie found a basket outside a gate. It belonged to Mrs Brown, who had just gone up the garden path to fetch her umbrella, and had popped her basket down for a moment, but Binkie didn't know this. He sniffed round the basket and wondered what it was doing on the path all alone.

He was an honest little dog and he thought he had better try to find the owner. But how could he do that? The basket didn't smell like anyone he knew.

"Well," thought Binkie, "the best

thing I can do is to take it to a policeman. Policemen are very clever, and one will be sure to know whose basket this is."

So he picked it up and off he ran, and on the way he met Scamp.

"Hello," said Scamp, in surprise. "What are you doing, Binkie? Playing errand boy?"

"No," said Binkie. "I found this basket on the path all alone, and I am taking it to a policeman to find out who owns it."

"What a silly thing to do!" cried Scamp. "Why don't you bite through those paper bags and see if there is anything nice to eat in the basket! That is what I would do."

"Oh no!" said Binkie. "The things belong to someone else, not me. Go away, Scamp! This isn't your basket. I shall bite you if you try any tricks."

"All right, all right," said Scamp. "I shall go and find a basket of my own. And I shan't let you share if I find any sausages or biscuits or bones in it! So there!"

He ran off to look for a basket. Binkie went on his way, and very soon he met a big policeman. He ran up to him and put the basket down at his feet. The policeman

was surprised. He bent down and picked it up. He felt among the parcels and found a bill made out to Mrs Brown.

"Why," he said, "these things belong to Mrs Brown! Did you find the basket, little dog? It was clever of you to bring it along to me. I will give it back to Mrs Brown."

Binkie trotted along beside him, pleased. When the policeman got to Mrs Brown's house he found her dreadfully upset, because she couldn't find her precious basket anywhere, and it was full of groceries. How pleased she was to see the policeman bringing it up the path!

"This clever little dog found it," said the policeman, "and what is more, he's a very honest little dog, Mrs Brown, for he brought it to me!"

"The dear, good, little chap!" cried Mrs Brown, and she ran indoors to get a bone. "Here you are, little dog. Take this bone home and enjoy it!"

"Woof!" said Binkie, and he joyfully ran off with the bone.

And how was Scamp getting on? Well, he hadn't been able to find a basket; but just outside the baker's he had seen a sack which had been left ready to be taken into the shop, and he at once dragged it off, away round the corner.

Then he bit a hole in it and put his head in to see what was there, and it was nothing but white flour for making bread! It got up Scamp's nose, and he sneezed hard. "Atishoo! Atishoo!" The flour flew out of the sack all over him, for his sneezing puffed it here, there, and everywhere! Scamp ran off, still sneezing, and then he thought he would like to see

what the baker said when he found his bag of flour gone! The little dog didn't know that he was covered with white flour from head to tail!

Well, the baker was very cross about his missing sack of flour, and as soon as he saw Scamp at the shop door, he knew quite well what had happened!

He made a dart at Scamp and caught the floury dog by the collar. He pulled him out of the shop and followed the floury footmarks down the street and round the corner till he came to his bitten sack! And then didn't he shake Scamp! Didn't he

shout at him! Scamp tried to escape and fell head first into the sack and rolled in the flour till he could hardly breathe!

"That will teach you not to steal bags of flour!" roared the angry baker, and let him go. Scamp ran home, sneezing and spluttering; and when he was nearly there he met Binkie, carrying his enormous bone. How surprised he was to see Scamp, white with flour, almost sneezing his head off!

"Look what I got for taking the basket back that I found," said Binkie.

"And look what I got for not taking back something I found," whined poor Scamp. "Honesty is best, Binkie, there's no doubt about it. Atishoo! Atishoo!"

Poor Scamp! Binkie gave him a bit of his bone – though he really didn't deserve it, did he?

The Christmas Pudding
That Wouldn't Stop

Gubbleup and Gubbledown were two little goblins and they lived in Gubble Cottage. They were both dressed exactly the same in little high caps, green tunics and green leggings, but you could never mistake one for the other, for Gubbleup was very tall and thin, and Gubbledown was very small and fat.

It was nearly Christmas time, and Gubbleup and Gubbledown had been to a great many parties.

"We really ought to give a party ourselves," said Gubbleup.

"Yes, we ought," said Gubbledown. "We've been to so many. What about having one tomorrow?"

"Have you got any money?" asked Gubbleup.

Gubbledown turned out his pockets.

"I've got two pennies and a halfpenny," he said. "That wouldn't go far towards paying for a party. How much have you got, Gubbleup?"

Gubbleup took down a little china pig from the mantelpiece and unscrewed its head. Inside were some pennies, halfpennies and a silver threepenny bit.

"One threepenny bit, three pennies and three halfpennies," he said.

"What does your money and mine make altogether?" asked Gubbledown.

"That's very difficult," sighed Gubbleup, taking a pencil from his pocket. "It's the sort of sum we did when we were at school. Now let me see – one threepenny bit, three pennies, three halfpennies, two pennies of yours and a halfpenny."

After a great deal of thinking and scribbling and rubbing-out, the goblins decided that they had exactly ten pence.

"Oh dear – that won't go far towards buying things to eat," sighed Gubbleup.

"We must have a Christmas pudding," said Gubbledown, firmly. "You can't have a Christmas party without a Christmas pudding."

"But how can we have a Christmas pudding?" asked Gubbleup. "They cost a lot of money – and besides, we don't know how to make one."

"Well, let's go and ask the old Sugarstick Gnome if he'll make us one for fivepence," said Gubbledown. "If he will, we can spend the other fivepence on jellies and cakes, and that will be enough for a party."

"The Sugarstick Gnome won't make one for fivepence!" said Gubbleup. "Don't be silly!"

"I'm not silly," said Gubbledown, offended. "Come on, and we'll see."

So the two goblins put on their pointed caps, and went through the wood to the Sugarstick Gnome's.

He lived in a funny shop, whose chimneys looked like barley-sugar sticks, and whose walls were as brown as chocolate. His pretty curtains had a pattern of cakes, tarts and sweets all over them, and altogether his shop was a most exciting one to visit.

The Sugarstick Gnome made puddings and pies, cakes and tarts, sweets and

167

chocolate. He had a little kitchen at the back of the shop, and here he made everything. No one knew how he made his goods, for he always kept his kitchen door shut and the curtains drawn tightly across the window.

There was never any smell of cooking at the shop of the Sugarstick Gnome. So people said that he made all his goodies by magic – but nobody knew exactly how.

Gubbleup and Gubbledown soon reached the shop, opened the door, and went in.

No one was there.

The two Goblins waited for some minutes, and then grew impatient.

"Wherever can the Sugarstick Gnome be?" exclaimed Gubbleup.

Gubbledown rapped on the counter.

Nobody came.

The kitchen door was shut, and no sound came from the kitchen.

"Perhaps the Sugarstick Gnome is ill," said Gubbleup at last.

"Shall we go into the kitchen and see?" asked Gubbledown.

"No," said Gubbleup. "He might

be cross. People say he has a very bad temper. We don't want to be turned into peppermint lumps or anything."

"Good gracious!" said Gubbledown, startled. "I should think not. But what can we do, Gubbleup? I'm getting tired of waiting here. And he may be ill, you know."

"Well, let's go and see if we can peep into the kitchen window," said Gubbleup, jumping off his chair.

So the two goblins ran out of the shop and went round the garden to the back window. The curtains were drawn tightly over the window – all but a little crack at one side!

"We could peep in through this crack!" whispered Gubbledown, and put his eye to it.

What he saw made him stare in astonishment.

The Sugarstick Gnome was not ill. He was making Christmas puddings. There they were, spread out in delicious rows on the table.

But dear me, he made them in a most extraordinary way!

The goblins saw him take up a tiny black currant and put it on a plate. Then he danced solemnly round it, and chanted an odd song:

> Little black currant of mine
> Make me a pudding, I pray,
> A Christmas pudding as fine
> As anyone's baking today!

Then right before Gubbleup's and Gubbledown's astonished eyes the currant seemed to swell, and gradually a fine plum-pudding grew up on the plate. It grew bigger and bigger and bigger, until it was as large as a pumpkin.

The two goblins were so surprised that they sat down on the grass outside and stared at each other.

"So that's how he makes all his things!"

whispered Gubbledown. "What powerful magic must be in that currant!"

"Let's peep again!" said Gubbleup. Once more the goblins put their eyes to the crack and looked.

The Sugarstick Gnome was just taking out the magic currant to use again for another pudding. Immediately the first pudding stopped growing.

The goblins watched him put the currant on an empty plate, and heard him sing the magic song again. Once more a pudding grew.

Gubbleup and Gubbledown didn't wait for the end of that one. They marched back into the shop, and stamped loudly on the floor.

"If he's got so many, surely he can sell us one cheaply," said Gubbledown, hoisting his fat little body up on a chair.

The Sugarstick Gnome came into the shop, and shut his kitchen door behind him.

"Good morning," said Gubbleup. "Would you please sell us a big Christmas pudding for fivepence?"

The Sugarstick Gnome laughed.

"No, I won't," he said. "Big puddings cost twenty pence."

"Oh dear," said the goblins in dismay. "Are you sure you couldn't?"

"Quite," said the Sugarstick Gnome. "Anything else you'd like?"

Gubbleup and Gubbledown were most disappointed.

"Oh well," said Gubbleup, sighing. "I suppose we'd better make do with cakes and jelly. How many can you let us have for ten pence?"

"One red jelly, two yellow jellies, six chocolate cakes, six cream buns, and twelve currant cakes," said the Sugarstick Gnome. "Very cheap, too."

"All right," said Gubbleup. "We'll call for them tomorrow at two o'clock. We're going to have a party in the afternoon, so please have them ready."

The goblins paid over their money and went out. They were so disappointed about the pudding that for a minute or two neither of them spoke a word.

Gubbledown heaved a sigh.

"It won't be much of a Christmas party

173

without a Christmas pudding," he sighed.

"No," said Gubbleup. "Still, we shall have twenty-four cakes and three jellies, and you know we've got a tin of chocolate biscuits."

"And we'll make some lemonade," said Gubbledown, cheering up. "And play lots of jolly games."

"Let's call and ask everybody now," said Gubbleup.

So the goblins called on their friends, and asked them all to come to their party the next day. Everyone was most delighted and accepted at once.

Then the two goblins hurried home and

cleaned up their living-room. They put holly all round the pictures, and made paperchains to go across the ceiling. That took them all the day, and they went to bed tired out.

Next morning they were most excited. Gubbleup made the lemonade, and Gubbledown got out the tin of chocolate biscuits and arranged them in nice little patterns on blue plates.

Then he got out all his best glasses and washed them ready for the party.

By that time it was a quarter to two, and the goblins thought they had better fetch the jellies and cakes from the Sugarstick Gnome's.

"Everybody's coming at three o'clock," said Gubbleup putting on his cap. "So we'd better hurry, Gubbledown."

Off they went through the wood, and reached the cake shop at just exactly two o'clock.

The shop was empty, and Gubbleup knocked on the counter.

Nobody came. Gubbleup knocked more loudly. Still nobody came.

Then Gubbledown saw a note on the

counter. On it was written:

Dear Gubbleup and Gubbledown,
I have to go out before two o'clock, but you will find your jellies and cakes in two big baskets under the counter.
From the Sugarstick Gnome.

The goblins ran round the counter to look for the baskets underneath. Sure enough, there they were.

Gubbleup stooped to get them, but he was so tall that he bumped against the kitchen door just behind him. It flew open. Gubbledown was just going to shut it, when he caught sight of something that made him stop.

He saw the magic currant all by itself in the middle of a plate on the kitchen table!

"Look! Look, Gubbleup!" he cried. "There's the magic currant!"

They stared at it – and the same naughty idea crept into their minds.

"Shall we borrow it, just for today?" whispered Gubbleup. "The Sugarstick Gnome's out, so we can't ask him if we may."

"We'll ask him afterwards," giggled

Gubbledown. "We'll take it back tonight and tell him we borrowed it. He can't say no then! We'll make a fine Christmas pudding for our party!"

The two rascally goblins picked up the currant, slammed the kitchen door, caught up their baskets and ran off.

"We'll give our guests such a surprise," grinned Gubbleup. "We'll let them see a Christmas pudding made before their eyes!"

The goblins hurriedly turned out the

jellies into pretty dishes, and spread out the cakes on their blue plates.

Right in the middle of the table they put a great big plate, and in the centre they placed the magic currant.

Soon the guests began to come, and very soon the party was in full swing. They played games and laughed until they were all out of breath.

"Now we'll have something to eat!" cried Gubbledown, leading the way into his bright little kitchen, where the meal was set out. Everyone took their places, and looked hungrily at the jellies, cakes and biscuits.

Then someone saw the empty plate on the table, with the little currant set in the middle.

"Whatever's that?" he cried.

Everybody looked. Gubbleup and Gubbledown laughed.

"Aha!" said Gubbleup, "that's a great surprise for you all, when you've eaten up everything else!"

Well, everybody was most puzzled. They couldn't think what the surprise could be, though they tried their very hardest. They

ate up all the biscuits and cakes, finished the jellies and drank the lemonade.

Then they waited to see what the surprise was.

"Watch!" said Gubbleup.

Then he and Gubbledown danced solemnly round the table, and sang the magic song:

> Little black currant of mine,
> Make me a pudding, I pray,
> A Christmas pudding as fine
> As anyone's baking today!

179

And as before the currant seemed to swell and a little pudding began to grow on the plate. How everyone stared!

"My!" they cried. "Good gracious! What a wonderful thing to be sure! A Christmas pudding growing before our eyes!"

"How do you stop it growing?" asked someone.

"That's easy!" said Gubbleup. "You just take out the magic currant, and the pudding stops at once!"

The pudding went on getting bigger and bigger. Soon it was the size of a cricket ball, then of a melon, then of a football.

"We'll let it grow just a little bigger," said Gubbleup. "It does look such a nice one."

They waited a minute longer, then they decided it was big enough.

Gubbleup bent over the pudding to take out the magic currant.

But oh dear me! All the currants looked exactly alike, and Gubbleup didn't know at all which was the one he wanted.

He picked out first one and then another – but he didn't get the right one, for still the pudding went on growing! He tried again, and Gubbledown helped him.

Not a bit of good! The pudding went on growing!

"Ha ha! Ho ho!" laughed everyone. "We shall all be able to have a great big helping, Gubbleup!"

The two goblins went on hurriedly picking out currants, hoping to come to the right one – and still the pudding went on growing.

It was bigger than the plate now, and little by little began to spread over the table. It grew as big as a pail – then as big

181

as a dustbin, then as tall as a pillar-box, but much wider.

The two goblins were getting frightened. Suppose they couldn't find the magic currant! Every minute was making it more difficult, for the pudding seemed to be getting fuller and fuller of currants!

The guests thought it was a fine joke. They thought Gubbleup and Gubbledown were giving them a great treat, and they longed to begin on the pudding.

"Yes, cut yourselves big slices!" said Gubbleup, suddenly thinking that the pudding would certainly be made smaller then. So everyone cut a huge slice and began eating.

But the pudding went on growing! Soon it reached the ceiling, and was squashed down flat. But that made it grow wider, and it was soon bigger than the table.

Then bits fell on to the floor, and made a dreadful mess. The guests began to think something really must be wrong. They felt afraid.

"Can you really stop the pudding growing?" asked one of them.

"No!" said Gubbleup, almost crying.

"Oh dear, oh dear, it will grow as big as this room, I do believe!"

"Gubbleup!" said Gubbledown in despair. "Let's go and ask the Sugarstick Gnome to stop it for us!"

"You go," said Gubbleup.

So off went Gubbledown and ran all the way. He burst into the shop, and to his great relief saw that the Sugarstick Gnome was home again.

The Sugarstick Gnome was looking

terribly cross. He frowned when he saw Gubbledown.

"Did you take my magic currant?" he thundered.

"Yes, yes," stammered Gubbledown, "we – we b-b-borrowed it, and now we c-c-can't stop the p-p-pudding growing. Would you come and take the currant away?"

"No!" said the Sugarstick Gnome. "You can keep it."

"Oh please, please, please!" begged Gubbledown. "The pudding will force our roof off, I do believe."

"What will you give me if I come?" asked the Sugarstick Gnome.

"We haven't any money," said Gubbledown, sadly.

"Well, will you both come and chop up firewood for me each day for a month?" asked the Sugarstick Gnome.

"Yes, yes, yes!" cried Gubbledown, "but please do come now!"

The Sugarstick Gnome went off with him. When they came to Gubble Cottage they saw the pudding bulging out of the window. It was so big that everyone had had to go out of the room. Poor Gubbleup was terribly afraid the walls would be broken down.

The Sugarstick Gnome wriggled into the room, and quick as a wink picked out a currant. At once the pudding stopped growing.

"Oh, thank you, thank you!" cried Gubbleup.

"You are two bad little goblins to borrow something without asking," said the Sugarstick Gnome. "I've a good mind to spank you both. Mind you come every day for a month and chop firewood for me as a punishment."

He stalked off. All the guests said good-

bye too, and went.

Gubbleup and Gubbledown stared at each other.

"The party's quite spoilt," said Gubbleup, sadly.

"It's our own fault," said Gubbledown miserably. "But oh, Gubbleup – what are we to do with that great pudding filling up our kitchen like that?"

"Eat it, I suppose," said Gubbleup.

The next day they went to chop firewood for the Sugarstick Gnome, and he kept them at it all the morning. For a month they worked for him, and very hard they found it.

But the horridest thing of all was eating the huge Christmas pudding. They got so tired of it that they vowed they would never touch another one all their lives long.

So if you ever meet two goblins who can't bear the sight of Christmas pudding, just ask them if their names are Gubbleup and Gubbledown!